To Stay
Alive

To Stay Alive

MARY ANN GRAVES AND THE
TRAGIC JOURNEY OF THE DONNER PARTY

SKILA BROWN

CANDLEWICK PRESS

Image of Mary Ann Graves on page 283 appears courtesy of California State Parks; Sutter's Fort SHP #6748.

First edition 2016

Library of Congress Catalog Card Number 2016946911
ISBN 978-0-7636-7811-1

16 17 18 19 20 21 BVG 10 9 8 7 6 5 4 3 2 1

Printed in Berryville, VA, U.S.A.

This book was typeset in Centaur.

Candlewick Press
99 Dover Street
Somerville, Massachusetts 02144

visit us at www.candlewick.com

For my father, Dwayne King

because like Franklin Graves, everything he does is for his family.
I have no doubt he would have gotten us through then.
He is always getting us through now.

Thanks, Dad. You're the best.

THE LACON HOME JOURNAL

April 7, 1846

LOCAL FAMILY HEADING WEST

Local resident Franklin Graves announced he'll be making the journey west later this spring, relocating his family to the better climate and lands of California. Making the trip will be:

Franklin Graves, 57

Elizabeth Graves, 45, wife

Sarah Fosdick, 21, daughter

Jay Fosdick, 23, son-in-law

Mary Ann Graves, 19, daughter

Will Graves, 17, son

Eleanor Graves, 13, daughter

Lovina Graves, 11, daughter

Nancy Graves, 7, daughter

Jonathan Graves, 6, son

Frank Graves, 4, son

Eliza Graves, infant, daughter

John Snyder, 25, hired hand

Mr. Graves wishes to sell his home and land. Interested parties should inquire with him soon.

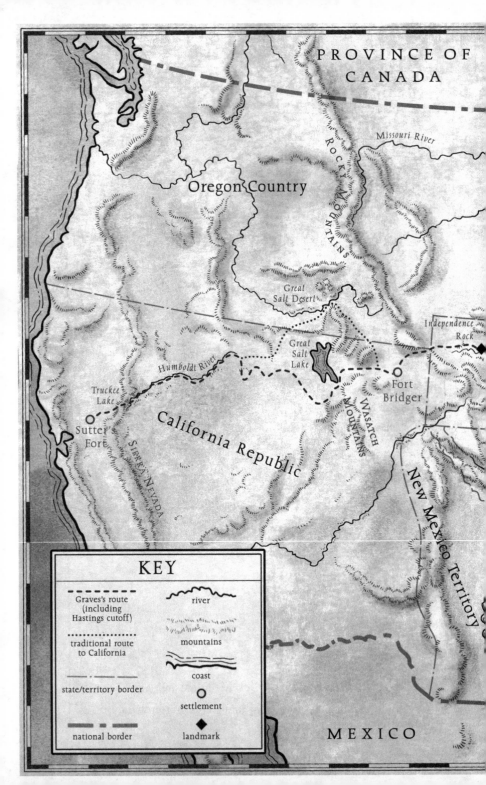

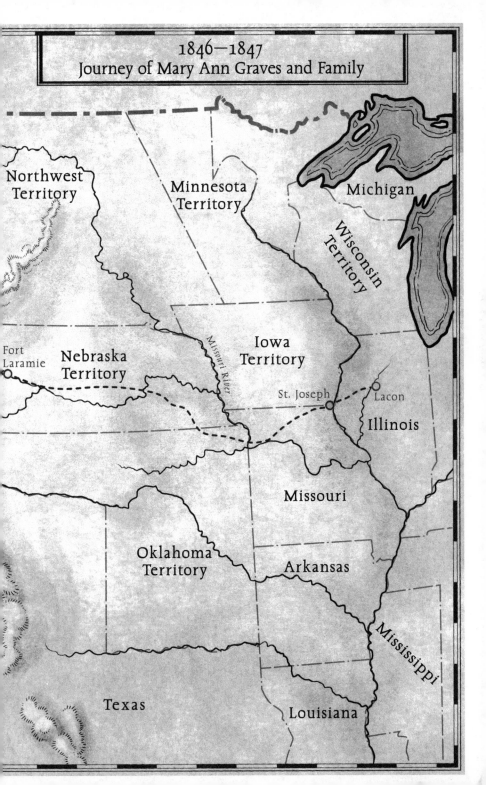

Spring
1846

New Dress

It's finished.
   The travel dress,
thick and crisp and green,
   white buttons in a line,
a bright stiff collar, perched high.
   It's a dress for an adventure,
a dress ready for
   whatever it will face.
Strongly stitched, unspoiled, new,
   well made.
It is meant to endure.

Empty Wagons

Two weeks ago they came,
wooden ribs arching up
on edge, designed to give structure
for the cover — great big stretch
of canvas — draped over, falling down,
curving around, like a frown.

Every time the wind blows,
the canvas, stretched tight,
cracks, like the sound of tree limbs snapping.
The wind goes right through
the empty wagons, shoots out the other side,
nowhere to linger.
As if the belly of the wagon
is bare, hollow, hungry.

Father

Father

has   been

burning   like   the   sun

for   weeks,   warming   any   sadness

about   leaving   that   anyone   else   had

creeping   up   before   it   could   properly   sprout.

It's spring but he hasn't filled his days with tired

planting. He's whistling. Cleaning his rifles, packing up

powder, his fingers itching to squeeze on the aim of some wild

meat in the west.   He has already abandoned his shoes,

even   though   the   ground   is   nowhere   near

summer   warm.   But   his   feet   are   hot

with   the   burn   to   walk,   to   ride,   to   move

west.   He   looks   like   a   wildfire,

burning   through   the   field,

and   we've   no   choice

but   to   circle   around

him.

Sarah

            She's impossible to hate, my sister, with her
always sweet pies,
always sweet words,
always kind heart.   Even her humility — "Mary Ann,
            you're much better at quilting than I" — is
always sincere.   Never mind that it's just a quilt,
            and who cares if I'm good at that anyway.

            She's
always first, my sister,
always two years ahead, seven times
            as smart, four steps in front, as though I can't go anywhere until
            she's cleared the way.
            The first one married, as of last month, even though she
always says, "Mary Ann, you're pretty enough to pick out any husband
            you'd want."   Even though boys have only seemed to grow
            on her side of the field.   But now,   things might be different,
            it might just be my turn, now that she's gone and made herself
            Mrs. Jay Fosdick.   Not as if I wanted Jay anyway — shorter
            than corn in June, plainer than a bare patch of land.
            I don't know why she's in a hurry for all that.
            All she has to do is turn around to see there's
always more family than a person really needs.

California

This place,   California,
is drawing Father west,   calling to him,
fertility of soil,   infinity of spring,
causing him to sell his land,   herd
his family through   two thousand miles
of wind,   deserts,   mountains,   storms,
land unclaimed,   wild   with danger
and game.   I cannot wait to see it
for myself.   Today Father comes home
from the courthouse,   having sold the cabin,
the land,   our home. I watch him open up
a sack of coins,   coins from Mexico,
France, Spain.   I run them through
my fingers while Jay and Father   cut holes
in a wooden board,   then we all drop
the coins in,   one thunk at a time.
Father will nail it   under one of the wagons
so no one will know it's there.   Nancy
says,   "What's so great about California
anyway?"   Father tells her how
it's perfect,   like a piece of heaven.
"Why don't we just   go to heaven instead?"
she asks.   Father only laughs,
but Mother says,   "No one gets to heaven,
child,   unless first   they've died."

We Wait

Even though he's itching to go,
Father says we wait.

Wait deeper into spring,
until the roots

in the ground along the way are closer
to moving, pushing

up, growing tall, sweet,
into food for our cattle,

wait as long as we dare, hoping
winter won't come and cool everything

before we have a chance to arrive,
before our five-month journey has ended.

There's only a little gap between rain and snow,
an open window of sunshine to go,

it all must be timed just right
or it will go all wrong,

like a cup of tea that slips
from too hot to too cold

without leaving enough time
in between to drink it.

Full Wagons

Father's traded for livestock,
animals that will walk the

1,900 miles,
3 horses to ride for scouting, hunting;
20 head of cattle to be milked, and then
slaughtered, eaten, along the way.
18 oxen to pull
3 wagons.
2 are filled completely—no room
for people—sacks and sacks
of flour, coffee, sugar, salt, dishes, forks,
spoons, candles, soap, guns, bolts of
fabric, tools for the new farm, spare parts for
the wagon.
1 is our home,
filled with chairs, 3 mattresses, a
lantern on a hook, everything
stacked like we've taken up residence
in a rickety, rolling root cellar.

We're traveling with all that we have, leaving
nothing behind, nothing tying us down, nothing
holding us back.
We have everything we need.

Good-bye

We go through town
when we depart. Lovina
cries, waves to the Nelson girls,
whom she won't see anymore
at school. Jay hugs his family,
who are all torn up.
Sarah cries, waves
to everybody. Will sits up high and tall on his horse, like a hero
returning from war.

I take one last look
at this dreary town and then bring up my hand to my mouth,
blow the loudest smack
of a good-bye kiss.

Eleanor looks over at me in shock,
but I just turn around, look away,
away to where we're going, where Father
has his eyes fixed, a big smile
stretched upon his face.

I toss Frank up on my shoulders, help his arm wave good-bye.
And I wave too.
> *Good-bye, Lacon.*
> *Good-bye, winters.*
> *Good-bye, childhood.*

That First Night

Nothing could be grander
than a big crackling fire
under a starry sky,
insects humming in the dark all around,
the sound of Jay moving the bow across his fiddle,
the smell of onions and potatoes
in the air—turned cool enough
to draw you closer to the flames,
close enough to see them dance
in the dark eyes of a new boy
who can't stop looking your way.

John Snyder

He heard that we were going, asked
to come along. Offering up
his help with the animals
in exchange for a place
along the way.

Eleanor says
he's handsome. Sarah says
he's capable. Will says
he's too firm with the oxen. Lovina says
he looks stronger than even Father. Jonathan says
he has curly hair like a girl. Nancy says
he walks like he's swinging. Frank says
he smells like vinegar.

He doesn't talk much,
even when Eleanor and Lovina trail after him,
pepper him with silly questions.

He walks up front with the oxen,
their tails swishing around,
his long whip dragging the ground.

He wears a face that is blank, serious, full of
mysterious thought,
and seems completely unashamed that his eyes
follow me wherever I go.

Days

Every day is easier than at home.
No same old chores,
seeds to plant,
floor to sweep.
No clothes to make,
weeds to pull,
feathers to pluck.

There's water to be hauled — but not far,
we stay beside the path of the river.
There's food to be cooked — but only twice,
we eat dried fruit, cold meat, and biscuits at noon to save time.
There's dishes to be cleaned — but quickly,
scrubbed with gritty sand, rinsed in water, wrapped in cloth
to keep the dust away.

Father tells us to be on the lookout for snakes, thieves,
storms, but my eyes stay straight ahead,
pointed toward California, where a better life awaits,
better than what we've left behind.

Nights

Extra canvas over wooden stakes makes
a tent beside the wagon, two places to sleep.

Inside the wagon we shift,   move,   rearrange.
                          "Careful of my doll," Nancy says.
Quilts brought out, some left in.
                          "There's no room," says Lovina.
A mattress out, some left in.
                          "Switch me sides," Eleanor says.
Food put away, inside.
                          "I forgot to fill the buckets," Sarah says.
Animals fed, watered, tied.
                          "It's not going to work," says Will.
Sticks stacked for the morning fire.
                          "He took my blanket!" Jonathan cries.
Bread in the coals to rise.
                          "Hand it back to him, Frank." Mother sighs.
Water gathered.
                          "I'm thirsty," says Frank.
Baby changed.
                          "No more talking," Father says.

Finally it's done.
Mother's found a place for each of us
to lie, John by the fire outside, the family
fitted in like puzzle pieces, no room
to move around.
Sarah says good-night, moves
to sleep with Jay in the tent beside the wagon,
where they'll have a bit of privacy
and lots more air to breathe.

Spring

At home
we work for spring,
wrench it out
of winter-hardened ground, begging
seeds to reach up, find us.
We implore it
into the cabin, opening the door, fetching
fresh air.

Here
we do not raise a hand, only travel by and watch it come to us, green
grass pushing up under yellow, birds finding their way,
flowers popping up, shy along the path,
as if west is spring and we
are riding into it.

As if here —
there never was a winter.

Father says spring will always be this easy,
at our new home in the west.

The Fire

John sits beside me every night
as we eat around the fire.
He talks more to Will or Jay, sometimes
Lovina, always in his shadow.
Tonight he turns to me.
     "How is it?"

The chunk of deer, warm,
crisp in my fingers, had just reached
my lips. I pull it back.
"It's good," I say. "Don't you think?"

I turn to Eleanor, beside me.
"You did well," I say.
"Did you use grease from the morning's bacon?"
Eleanor nods, looks at John. I open my mouth,
scrape my teeth up over the side, bite
into the sweetness. Before I can swallow,
John says,
     "I killed it, you know. One shot.
     Your pa was still loading his gun."

He's waiting for me
to say something, I can tell, but I don't know
what to say. And my mouth
is full of food. He watches me chew
for a minute, then turns to talk to Will.

"Mary Ann!" Eleanor whispers.
"You hurt his pride."

I swallow, shrug,
whisper back, "I didn't know
it was such a fragile thing."

Dinner

Next night, John's a holler's length away,
minding the cattle in a sweet spot of grass,
while the rest of us sit down to eat,
around the fire, by the trickling stream.

"Someone want to run him up a plate?" asks Jay
as he spoons out beans and ham.

I take a bite, chew,
as though I'm completely unaware
everyone watches me without looking my way.

There's a pause, one beat too long,
then Eleanor says, "I'll do it," casual but quick.
She moves her plate out of her lap,

but I'm up
and halfway to the pot of food
before she can even stand, before
I even realize I'm going,
as if my legs are somehow connected
to her brain.

A Plate

I walk to him with this plate and try
to think of what I'm going to say — something
sweet, something funny, something wise.

"I'm glad you're here," I say, once I'm standing
before him. "I'm glad Father needed some help
and you wanted to come. I'd probably be the one
up here by myself stuck minding the cattle if you
weren't here, so thanks."

      John blinks, nods, seems a little confused.

I hand over the plate. "Father says you're a good worker,"
I say, because I can't stand the silence. "Says you're
earning your keep — even if you do eat a lot."
I wait for him to laugh but he

      stops chewing and stares, says, "I do more
      work than he does." His face is tight now,
      the space between us all wrong.
      "I'd get us there faster, too," he says
      with a scowl. "If I were in charge."

I tilt my head, feel my mouth open
before I can stop it. "Well, you'd have to have money
and something to your name
to actually be in charge, though, wouldn't you?"

      John stops chewing again and stares.

I turn as quickly as I can, fast to walk away.

Well.
That's the end of that.

A Quilt's Beginning

I climb into the rear of the wagon,
where it's stuffy, bumpy, cramped,

but where I can take out the sewing basket,
push some thread through a needle, tuck it

into my stiff left sleeve, where it will be safe
until I need it. I sort through piles of scraps,

corners of blues, greens, a triangle of yellow,
left-behinds from quilts put together before.

But mostly there is red, bits of Mother's rust-colored dress,
her Sunday best, that she wore for years, cut up

before we left. "Won't need to look fancy
for the trip," she said. "I'll make a new one once we're settled."

Faded fabric pieces, some worn thin,
some darker, thicker, all cut

into big squares. I unfold one, spread it out
onto my lap.   And I can see it, this quilt, laid out on a hill,

strips of faded red sewn together like a sunset,
little bits of blues, yellows, greens in between.

I know how I will sew it.
I pick up the piece in my hand, cut a tilted line.

Rain

The rain comes,

falls on my dress,

makes dots of bright green that bleed

together till the whole thing's wet.

Every day has rain,

and there is no house

for cover, no place

to stay dry, no way

to escape it.

Mud

Frank has found a new plaything.
He brings me mud pies,
mud cakes, mud loaves of bread he's baked,
as though he's playing at being a girl.
I pat his shoulders, pretend to eat each one.
Mud lingers on my cheeks, my lips,
causes Mother to frown, Father to laugh,
Frank to smile in delight.

"Really, Mary Ann," Eleanor says,
which I ignore.   It's not like
it doesn't cover us anyway, head to toe.
This mud   squelches under oxen hooves,
                  splatters the wagon,
                  dots our dresses,
                  dries on our stockings,
                          makes them crisp, stiff as bones,
                  hides in our hair,
                  paints the wagon wood.

I smell it at all times,
hear it all day,
        taste it every time I chew.

Wheels

Sometimes a wheel gets stuck in the mud,
deep, wet and thick,   will not budge.
The oxen strain, the wagon pulls,
but the wheel is firmly planted.
Today this happens while Will and Jay are away, scouting,
Father and John out of earshot in the lead.

"Let's get it out ourselves," I call to Sarah, but she's already
gathering up her skirts, darting off toward the front, to get a man.

Eleanor, beside me, sucks in a breath, walks clear
of where the wheel is spinning splatters of mud out, around.

I tell Nancy and Jonathan, "Get behind the wheel. Push
as hard as you can."   Digging my heels deep into the squelch,
I pull on the slippery wood, paint my sleeves with brown as I do.

After three heaves, the wagon moves.
I step away, search for a clean corner of my apron
to wipe the mud from my eyes,
but the apron is covered in brown.

"Mary Ann!" Sarah says, out of breath. "You've ruined your dress!"
She's staring at me, her mouth wide open, Father and John at her side.

I know my dress will never be
the same, but it feels good to surrender
to it, stop trying to pretend I could stay clean.

John's face looks disgusted. But Father
laughs, says, "You got it, then?"

I nod, fling some mud from my sleeves,
smile.

Closer

Nights are cold but shorter.
Days are getting longer,
warm enough that nooning means finding shade,
that my morning shawl
is off before we even start walking,
that sweat gathers
in the band of my bonnet,
from my forehead to my ears.

There are houses now,
farms, cabins closer together,
almost to St. Joseph, the city by the river.
We've been walking for six weeks,
May's about to end. Still,
we've so much more to go.

Bitten

Frank screams a frantic cry, everyone runs
to him, but it's me who finds
the marks on his leg—snakebite.

Jay looks for the snake,
Sarah looks for water,
Will looks ahead for a house,
       in case we need some help.
       Eleanor says to me, "Weren't you
       looking after him?"
Father looks down at the bite, at the snake that Jay killed,
       says, "There, now. Not poisonous.
       It will be all right."
Frank squeezes my hand tight,
I suck in a breath so big I pop
a button on my dress
and let it lie.

Silent

I don't say much
as we get closer
to the town of St. Joseph.

I don't let go
of Frank's hand.

Camp

We pass through the town; words buzz by.
"Spring rush is over . . . the last of the stragglers here now . . ."
". . . more rain this spring than ever . . ." ". . . highest sales here yet . . ."

We make our way toward the outskirts,
where campfires dot dark's arrival;
more words buzz.
". . . making better time than I'd imagined . . ."
                    ". . . not as hard as I had heard . . ."
        "We'll arrive long before the weather cools . . ."

This camp is filled with bustle,
pots being scrubbed,
    animals being fed,
        food being cooked.
Teamsters are cleaning their guns,
    sharpening knives and axes.
        Sounds of mules braying, children playing,
                weave in and out, the air smells
                        of bread baking, bacon frying.

We make our camp, cook our meal. Father strides off
to find some others traveling in our direction,
a group we can join.
            "There's safety in numbers," Will explains to me.
            "Better if we travel together."

I nod, but I'm not thinking about safety, only
the adventure
of traveling among this field of new faces.

In the Dark

In the dark
people walk to a large campfire
where many families gather.
Jay and three others play
fiddles, someone has a flute.
In the dark, boys
ask me to dance.   I spin
again and again in arms, arms, arms.   In the dark,
they can't see my filthy dress, and I can't see
their faces, but I know,
I can tell,   that none of them
is John.

Clicking

I lie in the wagon,
beside Eleanor's snores, wait
for sleep to come,
but my thoughts are stuck on
that last night at home, in the bed Sarah and I shared,
her whispering to me what Jay said
when she told him we were leaving.

Since I laid eyes on you, Sarah Graves,
all I wanted was
to call you Mrs. Fosdick,
to fall asleep beside you,
to get old and die inside your arms.

Outside I hear crickets,
chirping in and out,
a never-ceasing clicking,
like the ticking of a clock.

Summer

Morning

Morning means
shaking off sleep, shaking out blankets,
shaking Lovina and Eleanor, lying beside me, awake.

Morning brings
Mother's voice piercing through the quiet.
"Eleanor, water the horses. Lovina, change the baby.
Mary Ann, gather up the bread out of last night's fire."

My hands are stiff, cold,
quick to burn, when I reach in,
grab the bread that's been rising all night.
Sarah slices bacon with a knife,
Mother's stirring hominy grits.

I smell coffee brewing
from somewhere close by,
where the sounds of others waking reach us,
cause us to move a little faster,
as though we're suddenly running behind.

Morning brings
rounds of negotiations
as the men settle the order of our wagon line.

I do not see how this matters one bit

until we get going

and the dust of those ahead
makes it impossible to see.

Our Business

This place has no cover,
stretches wide like a mocking smile,
not even a tree or rock or bush to duck behind
when you need to relieve
yourself. Like animals,
we go, off to the side
of the dust and the crowds and the talking and walking.
Ladies to the left.
Gents to the right.
Sarah says at least our skirts hide
our business from sight
but I can't put enough space between my body
and my skirt to keep it from
getting ruined.

Wide

Days pass by, fields pass by.
When we can, we spread out
our wagon train,

w i d e,   w i d e,   w i d e,

move in a line, stretched side to side,
the length of a mile,
so it looks like we're all diving ahead
in a race to see   who gets there first.

Buffalo

They dot the slope
beside where we ride,
their heads all bowed west,
like ripples stitched in a quilt,
like the scales on the side of a fish.
They appear as soft and gentle as a field full of petals,
with a shagginess that hangs friendly as Father's beard.

Lovina and Nancy have made a contest
of who can gather up the most chips.
Eleanor holds her basket up high, waist level, her elbows pointed
out.   "Just think, Mary Ann," she says, the voice
of maturity. "One day our children
will beg us to tell the story again of how we
filled up our baskets with buffalo chips,
used them to grow our fires, roast our dinner."

I am tired of these beasts, tired
of the smell of their waste burning while we cook our food, tired
of the taste of their meat.
All the dried meat we have in the wagons—I wonder why
we need more. But Father says that stash
is not for the journey but for the winter
that lies ahead,
which makes no sense because
if California winters are as mild as we have heard,
we'll find plenty to eat when we arrive.

Edward Trimble

Last night, Pawnees sneaked
into our camp, drove away some cattle,
without a sound.
Over one hundred head.

All of ours are still here, but Father,
Will, and John go out with the men
to find the missing beef.
Midday they're back, only
a smattering of beasts behind them, faces knotted
with bad news.

A man,   Edward Trimble,   is dead.

Indians tried to steal
his horse; they shot him.
The horse, alive, carries his body
slung over its back.

John is yelling about revenge, but Father silences him
with a glare as
heaviness spreads over all of us.
Trimble's widow gathers her children, all
small, around her and sobs
with only her eyes.

She is big with another child
and now with so much more.

His Widow

The men bury him late in the day.
Father and Jay help.

His widow, Abarilla,
is not there.

She's going through the camp, before dark arrives, asking,
begging, for a way to go home.

There are some men — good men — going east
who say they'll take her.

Chop her wood, drive her cattle, mend her
wagon wheels.   But they are only men.

She looks at them, her hand on a belly
about to burst from burden,

then eyes the sky, where the clouds are capturing the last light
from the sun and rolling away, taking it with them.

She gives her head the slightest,
saddest shake as she walks on.

For she needs women — other women — to help her
birth the child inside her

and all the women
are going west.

Ahead

Father returns from scouting, says
we'll reach Fort Laramie by dark.
People cheer because there'll be trading,
because this is the last official stop,
because tomorrow is the Fourth of July,
the birthday of our nation, seventy years old.
Mother wants days of rest, shade.
Father says there will be men headed east, men who've come
from where we're going.
Lemonade for the children, whiskey for the men.
Everyone walks faster at the idea
of a few days' break.
I am walking so fast Frank starts whining
that he can't keep up. So I throw him on my back,
try to gallop.

Fort Laramie

My first glimpse
is all high walls.
Like a painting of a castle.

But closer, I see
it's only a tall fence.
I stare at it, take it in, wonder
what kind of bad needs a barrier that high.

Our group moves inside, where
many caravans are parked, camped,
cooking, smells of coffee brewing, pies baking.
Feels like St. Joe,
except here
everything is heavy, dusty,
tired,   slow.

Fourth of July

A day of resting, mending,
packing, restacking.

Horses are brushed, oxen unyoked,
animals tied to stakes in the ground, left still, while we mill about.

There are sweet cakes and sweet drinks, advice
traded like goods. Descriptions of places we've been, places

we're about to see. Mother sends me to gather wood. I walk
around the edge of the fort, taking it all in. Everyone looks tired,

writing letters, washing skillets. Children reach into brambles
though the bushes appear worn out,

worn down, from many hands
reaching in over many days.

Scraps of talk weave into my ears
as I walk across the camp. Men, bent over maps, arguing over

Oregon — *Shorter trip! Family there. No war!*
versus California — *Better climate! Richer soil! Destiny to expand!*

Over oxen trades — *too skinny . . . worth more'n that . . . can't do any better,*
hired hands — *changed my mind . . . been six times . . . won't do it for free!*

Over the path to take — *proven route's for me . . . faster below the lake . . .*
man named Hastings says the cutoff will save three weeks!

Saving three weeks sounds good to me.
I'm tired of walking.

That Night

"We'll take the shortcut, pass south
under Salt Lake," Father says
that night around the fire. "Plenty of time
to cross the Sierra Nevada before
the end of fall."
Mother asks, "Who else is going?"
Father swats at a fly, replies, "No one
from here. They'll all be going north.
But there's a group ahead. If we leave tomorrow,
we should be able to catch up."
Mother doesn't answer but I do.
　　　"It's a good plan," I say. "The sooner, the better."
Mother gives me a strange look, but Father only smiles.
"Had enough of this adventure, have you?" he says.
　　　I shake my head. "This isn't an adventure.
　　　It's a journey of monotony and dust and sore feet."
Father laughs and laughs.
　　　I say, "I'm ready for California.
　　　To be at the foot of those mountains.
　　　That's when the adventure
　　　truly will begin."

Father doesn't say anything.
His smile lingers,
even though his laugh
has died.

Alone

We leave the fort as the sun is rising,
and then

there's open land.

It's only our family again,
plus John. No caravan of people. It is quiet enough
to hear the wagon wheels squeaking out a rhythm
as we move slowly
through this flat place,
this suffocating sameness.

Same

Hard to feel excited
about walking, walking, nothing but
walking, when everything looks the same,
when we run out of
landmarks, have no idea
if we're heading in the right direction,
heading anywhere at all.
Hard to tell if we're making progress or if one day
is just another's reflection.
So tired of all this walking
that when Frank whines
about his feet hurting, I say I don't mind
riding with him for a bit. Anything
for something different.
Even the stuffy wagon
seems like a welcome change of pace.

Inside the Wagon

never   still   never

                                     smooth

always   bump   shake   rattle

tossing   me   about

                    shaking   me   up   like   it
     wants   me   out

                                        can't   breathe

in this thing
          so crowded   and   dusty   and   filled

     no room   for   air   all of   our things   hanging and
piled   and crammed
                              getting   shaken around

                                   looking at me

like   they   do   not   belong   in   a   wagon

     out   in   the   middle   of

                                        nowhere

Days Passing

Days are passing by.

Nights.   Land.

But it's all the same.

Sometimes I sew

in the wagon, hooped quilt in my lap,

thick now with batting and backing,

making me hot but blocking the dust.   I stare

out the back, nothing

but scraggly bushes shoving their way up

through dry, cracked ground. I watch the space

we're leaving behind,

the painful,

plainful sameness.

Everyone

We're eating dried apples, brown and shriveled, oversweet,
when Jay spills a bit of coffee. Mother yells,
"Don't waste it!" It was the last of our supply.
She's angry now, all the time, the heat
taking away any spoonful of patience she had.
Eliza squirms, cries in her arms as we walk. Behind her, Jonathan's
covered with puffs of dust that he kicks up with his dragging feet.
"I'll take Frank," Eleanor says, holding out a hand
so she can hold on to his, avoid a turn holding the baby.
Frank sees through her plan, clings to me.
Nancy and Lovina are hot and miserable, tired
of walking, complain about their feet.
John does not glance my way.
Will spends all his time on a horse, scouting ahead, an excuse
to ride fast enough to feel a breeze.
Sarah talks to me constantly, brings me into conversations
with Jay, but I can't stand one more remark
about the weather, the land, the sky.
And there is nothing else to see.
Father laughs off Eleanor's complaints, whistling,
hurrying, suddenly anxious for a quicker pace.

"Won't be long now," he says to me, at noon, his arm around
my shoulder. "Maybe eight more weeks. Thank the Lord."

"Thank the devil," I say, jabbing him in the side.
"For getting us there so fast."

Father throws back his head and laughs,
his beard moving up and down,
up and down, with his chin.

It's impossible to be mad at him,
even when I want to be.

Emptying

Grass is no longer
everywhere. It's getting harder
to find food for the animals that drive us,
as if the land
is as tired as we are,
emptying itself, drained.

Frank brings me weeds, dry enough to crackle
in his fist. He calls them flowers.
I pat his shoulder, pick him up,
give his legs a break.

Nancy stomps
on the hard, cracked earth,
says she's tired of walking, tired
of walking, tired of walking,
asks once again why
we had to move west.

No one bothers answering.
Mother doesn't even stop walking,
because she knows Nancy has no choice
but to catch up. Waiting here for something better
isn't an option.
The only thing we can do is walk.

Independence Rock

Father says that's it for sure, a sign
our path is right.
A giant rock, smoothed-over top,
that lies up ahead.

"Lovely, isn't it?" asks Sarah.

"Like a giant pile of horse manure," I say.

"Really, Mary Ann," she says. But I hear her smile.

We watch it get larger
as the day moves on, as we get closer,
stopping to make our camp when we are right beside it,
where the fire pits we find are proof
of people who've camped here before.

Sarah and Jay run ahead to carve their names
on the stone. Will, John, Lovina follow right behind.
I take Frank from Mother as she leaves to gather wood.

"You aren't going?" she asks.
I shake my head.

Frank and I find some shade,
watch them all scamper up the sloping sides
of this giant mound of rock, searching for a place
to leave their names behind.

Frank asks, "Why's it called Independence Rock?"
I say, "People call it that because usually
they reach this place around Independence Day."

He starts to make a pile of dirt and I'm left
to take in the scattered remains
of two weeks ago, what's left behind

on the ground from whoever came before us,
whoever reached this place at the time that is deemed right.
Scattered fire pits, a broken chair, some sticks stuck in the ground
to mark a spot.   I don't know why.

It feels like we're arriving at a party in time
to clean up, after everyone's gone.
I feel worry start to move my fingers, make me twitch,
like the way it coils up in a nervous dread
when you're walking to school knowing you're late,
waiting for that moment when you walk in and everyone stares.

But I shake it off, remind myself
of the people behind us in Fort Laramie,
of the warm days that surround us, of how Father
always knows what to do.

Fort Bridger

Hardly a fort,
couple of log cabins,
an afterthought corral.

A withered mountain man,
Jim Bridger, says Hastings himself, the man who found the trail,
is up ahead, waiting to lead us,

says another group — thirty wagons
or so — just came through last week,
says yes, the shortcut is safe —

fine level road, plenty of water
and grass — it will save us
so much time,

says we'll beat the others on the northern path,
join up again at Humboldt River
weeks ahead of them,

says we'll reach Captain Sutter's fort
in California
in less than six weeks,

says all this as he sells us flour,
salt, coffee at three times
the prices we paid in St. Joe.

He smiles.

Wagons Ahead

I'm riding in the wagon, quilting in the heat,
only two days after
when I see
wagons circled up ahead.

Sarah says, "That can't be them already."

"They were a week ahead," says Jay.

But it is.
We move toward them,
where they stay still,
camped, in the middle of the day.

The Donner Party

They greet us,
  circling around,
    ask us where we're headed,
      tell us the land ahead looks rough,
        thick with brush, rocks, clogged with hills,
          tell us Hastings is leading another group
            ahead, tell us they've sent a man
            named Reed, two others on to fetch him,
              bring him back, show us a way through. They count
          the people in our party,
        the number of strong backs.
    They greet us,
  circling around.

James Reed

Out of breath he arrives,
says he found Hastings, obligated
to lead another party through,
cannot turn back for us.

Mr. Reed rides his horse tall, walks
about tall, talks with words tall, tall, tall.
His beard and hair are trimmed. His hat,
his coat, seem to repel the dust around them.
He has a forehead that is always bent to listen.
Even when he's the only one talking.

The others stand around him, listen to what he says.
His wife and children bob their heads like feeding hens.
But the rest of the party keep their distance,
wear their frowns, exchange glances
with one another. Glances I do not miss.

Talk begins among the men. "What choice do we have?" "We must
press on." "Winter's coming soon. We don't want to spend it here."

The women speak up too.   "... should turn around ..."
"... cold coming soon ..."   "... never make it through ..."

George Donner pats his wife on the back,
says, "Let's take a vote."

> They decide,
> these men,
> we will
> proceed.

This Party

They say George Donner is in charge,
even though it's James Reed on the horse,
pointing in the air to where the path should be.

I've clutched so many logs against my dress
its green can no longer be seen.
My sleeves are a shade of gray
born from hands dipped
in work.

While we work, the young girls talk,
      "Reed's a rich man, a merchant . . ."
"The Donners are rich too . . . expensive fabrics, piles of goods . . ."
     "That Mr. Keseberg . . . the one who beats his wife . . ."
        ". . . that widow woman from Tennessee . . ."

Everyone I stand next to has something to say,
and I wonder what they're saying about the Graveses.

Mrs. Bill McCutchen

There's a married woman, about my age,
with a baby daughter
and a worried face.

> "They aren't back yet," she says.
> "They should have arrived."

Someone doing laundry beside me in the creek whispers
to Lovina and me, explains this woman's
husband, Bill, and another man, Charles Stanton,
had gone with James Reed to find Hastings.
Their horses exhausted, the two men stayed on
another day with Hastings, to rest and then return.

Four days have passed
since Mr. Reed returned.

Other women around Mrs. McCutchen shush her,
squeeze her arm, tell her they're sure he's fine,
tell her they know any second now,
we'll hear the call of their return.

I watch her, absently smiling at these assurances,
think to myself, *Who knows*
where those men are now?

Women start walking to camp from the creek,
laundry gathered in their hands.
I add the last of my stack to the basket at Lovina's feet.

"Go ahead," I say. "I'll be there in a minute."

She frowns, takes the basket, walks away.
I turn to the woman, who's shifted
her baby to the other side, is leaning over
to pick up the basket, wedge it on her other hip.

"Here," I say. "Let me."
I reach out for the basket,
but she mistakes my arms' intentions,
hands me the child instead.

"Thanks," she says,
picking up the basket with both hands.

We turn, move to walk toward the camp.

"I don't know what I'll do,"
she says. "If he doesn't come back."

I shift the baby to the other side, turn to her,
say, "You'll keep doing
what you're doing now, Mrs. McCutchen.
The laundry, the cooking,
watering the cattle.
Nothing will change if he doesn't return."

Her steps slow a bit,
I peer over at her face.
She's shocked at what I said.
Maybe what she wanted
to hear was he was coming soon,
not to worry, he'd be here any day.
But it's too late for that now.

"I'm sorry," I say. "I only meant—"

But I stop because her head is slumped down,
her shoulders shaking and—oh—I've made her cry.

"Oh, no," I say, stepping toward her, reaching out
with my arm. "No, please don't—"

She looks up and I see
she's laughing.
Shaking her head now,
smiling, laughing.

"You're right," she says. "Exactly right.
I'll be fine."

I step aside,
shift the baby once again,
nervous now to open my mouth at all.

"Thank you," she says and sighs.
"Thank you for saying that."

I nod, set my body to walking,
not really sure what it was I did.

"And please," she adds.
"Call me Amanda."

Amanda

She does not seem put off by what I said, this girl.
She's suddenly beside me while I work,
bringing beef to add to our stew,
leaving her baby, Harriet, with our baby, Eliza,
on the quilt in the shade of our wagon,
where Eleanor and Lovina take turns
minding the babies and Frank during the day.

She's tough, this one.
Not afraid of hard work, speaking her mind,
joining in with others.
I learn she's from Missouri,
the oldest of eight children,
and hopes she doesn't have that many for herself.

Evenings

In a camp with others means evenings
are more lively.
Jay finds his fiddle, people
dance and sing.
I watch John stomp his feet on the planks of a wagon,
girls clap along from below.
I do not join in.
I've had enough of boys.

In between the dancing,
there are stories.

And it means later
lying there on the mattress in the wagon I can hear
people talking, dogs barking, babies crying,
sometimes more than babies.

One man beats his wife.

The rest of us
pretend
not to hear.

Keseberg

His name is Louis Keseberg,
six feet tall, a wide face,
tiny little eyes.

Thin red veins web his face,
as if he's trying to catch some prey,
or maybe it's an extra kind of containment,
as if his skin is not enough.

Last night the beating sounds
were loud enough
they echo in my ears this morning,
as I walk toward the path to clear.

I'm not the only one.
I see Mr. Reed, off his horse, speaking sternly to Keseberg,
hear him say, ". . . not a Christian thing to do . . ."
I quickly look away. But not before I catch a glimpse
of Keseberg's face, his eyes narrowed, his jaw
clenched so tight that his beard
sticks out like a spear.
And I know, somehow,
that Mr. Reed might have thought he was helping
that man's poor wife,
who is round with another child,
but he has made it worse.

Two Men

Next day there's a holler, loud,
from men up ahead.
I raise up at the waist, from where I was bent over
trying to wriggle out a boulder.
The yell is passed from one man to another,
as though it's sliding down the line of felled trees,
being pulled away by an ox,
a yell like they've found
something, discovered something.
I push the hair that's fallen in my face
inside my bonnet, where it stays,
stuck wet with sweat.
                    "What do you think it is?" Amanda asks, beside me.
"A path, I hope," I say.
"Already cleared and flat and—hey!"
I step forward, following Amanda,
who gasped, darted up the hill.
"Amanda?"
But she doesn't stop.
She walks faster,
her arms swinging slightly at her side,
almost running now.
I move my eyes on up ahead,
take in what she sees.

Oh, my.

Two men stand like scarecrows,
one a foot taller than the other,
gathering people around,
ragged clothes, dirty heads.

The tall one opens out his arms to her,
wide, calls out, "Amanda!"

Their Story

They say they got lost
making their way back,
their horses had run off,
two days without eating
anything.   They say the group ahead,
the group with Hastings, has more men,
fewer wagons to carry over this terrain.

They say for us — it's impassable.

Amanda takes the tall one's arm,
leads him down the hill.
                    "Let's get you some food," she says.
Everyone stays frozen
in place,
as if their warning
made our feet
too heavy to move again.
                    "Mr. Stanton," Amanda calls
                    to the other crumpled man,
                    "come along. I've stew for you as well."
The shorter man nods,
follows her down the hill, in a daze.
                    "Mary Ann," Amanda calls
                    over her shoulder, not bothering to turn around.
                    "Can you help me, please?"
I follow her down the hill,
leave those somber faces behind,
passing John, who doesn't see me
as he throws down the ax in his hand, lets it slice
into the ground, as he stomps his foot, swears out loud,
his face twisted with rage.

Mr. Stanton

Amanda stirs the soup, now simply beef and broth,
as all the onions and potatoes have long been eaten up,
in between our two wagons, underneath
where we've strung a rope, tied up the wet clothes
to dry in the sun. She's bouncing the baby, running
a warm cloth over her husband's face.
She asks me to add in more beef, asks me to fetch
more water to be warmed for the rags,
and before I know it, I'm helping Mr. Stanton
out of his coat.

He's a short man, about my height.
His clothes, though dirty, are fine and well made.

"He's a bachelor," Amanda says,
as if explaining why no woman had come running
up with rags, clothes, stew.
I am shaking out dust from his coat,
beating on the sleeves,
when he turns to me, says,
"It is my only flaw."

His beard widens a little and I know
there's a smile there underneath.
I smile, hand over his drink.

He says, "Thank you," before he even takes a sip.
The clothes flap between us
like a curtain that can't make up its mind.
I watch him eat, this man—not a boy—
blowing on the spoon before each bite,
his back held up straight on the stool.

An Argument

Tonight there is no dancing.
The men gather round one fire, argue
about what to do.
The women circle   behind.

Bill, Amanda's husband, is talking loudly,
talking often, giving warning. "No way
for wagons to go through this canyon . . . ahead is too steep,
the wagons will flip . . . no way to clear the path . . ."

> "Now, now," Mr. Reed says. "We can clear it
> if we all work together."

Bill says, "The wagons will be shattered and the oxen will be dead."

Other men mutter
to each other. I see John speak to Father,
agitation on his face.

> "What else can we do?" a man named Eddy says.
> "We've come this far, what else can we do?"

> > "We could turn back," a woman says.
> > Mrs. George Donner.
> > "Go to Bridger's Fort. Take the northern pass.
> > Follow the Humboldt River."

The men buzz at this, disapproval
crackles like the flames.
John stands, stomps off and away.

> > "That would be ridiculous," says Mr. Reed.
> > "It would add weeks onto our trip."

The men are silent, as if no one

wants to admit
they agree with him.

        "What do you think, Stanton?" Father asks.

Mr. Stanton sits on a chair pulled away from the others.
He takes out a long thin pipe from his mouth,
clears his throat, speaks. "There is another way.
A canyon to the north of here, might
be easier to pass."

Donner turns to Bill, who nods his head
reluctantly.   The men talk low
to each other. I see Mrs. Donner put her hand
on her husband's shoulder,
watch him pat it,
the way I do with Frank.

"Let's do that, then," Mr. Donner says.
"We'll start in that direction in the morning."

I turn to Sarah, standing beside me,
sigh. "We'd better get some sleep."

In the Canyon

Another day of hacking,
           clawing, chopping, making a path of empty
           inside this nest of growth.
           Slicing trees, moving boulders, hauling brush
           from here to there. Everyone is
toiling,   slashing, clearing. So much work in one day.
           So little space cleared away.
           Chiseling out the forest,
           severing this life,
           grinding away at time.   Trees

           bitten, bushes

           chewed, the woods get

           eaten, days get

           swallowed.

                    Thorns find their way
                    to my skin as if
                    my dress had holes in wait.

Each time I push on a rock, I think
that these men in our camp
cannot admit when they're wrong.

Each time I snap off a limb, I think
that those men at the fort
did not know a shortcut, had us make one instead.

Each time I pick up a load of brush that scratches my face, I think
how much easier it will be for those who come
next year, now that we've made a path.

Charles Stanton

He appears
sometimes beside me, as if the brush close to my body
calls to him to be carried away.
I do nothing to discourage this. I don't
spit or injure his pride or say something foolish or harsh.
I say almost nothing at all.
     I work.
     I carry sticks.
     I move rocks.
     I sweat.
     I bleed.
He doesn't always speak,
but when I look up, he
is often here.

His Pipe

Today, while we noon in the shade,
I watch him smoke his pipe,
something he does every time he sits.
The skin around his eyes relaxes each time he brings it to his lips.
The smell of his smoke lingers on my dress,
it's a welcome change.

He's describing a bird but I'm mesmerized
by the smoke that lingers
between us.
So I say, "Can I try that?"

He stops talking, his eyes get wide,
then his mouth stretches to meet them.
He hands me the pipe. I grab on to its warm, smooth bottom,
bring it up to my mouth. Charles says, "Now, what you want to do—"

Before he can finish, the stem is
between my lips,
I suck in smoke, swallow.
Fire and ash in my insides!

I pull out the pipe, cough,
cough, cough. Charles takes it,
says, with the kindest
chuckle, "You don't swallow it, Miss Graves."

I'm still coughing when he hands me
some water. I feel like fire
is inside me, trying to get out, making my nose run,
my eyes water, my stomach churn.

"Here," says Charles, handing me the pipe. "Try again.
This time sip it

like hot coffee. Leave it in your mouth, count to ten, then slowly
let it escape."

I am not sure I want to taste this again,
but I am sure I don't want to turn away,
so I take the pipe from Charles, bring it
to my lips, do exactly what he says.

And it's still fire, ash,
smoke, burning wood. But also the hot fruity mix
of apple and cherry, when you bite into a pie
that hasn't yet cooled.

I let out the smoke, give back the pipe, smile
at Charles, who's smiling right at me,
both of us sharing
this taste.

Finished

It takes us   eleven days
       to clear a path,
move enough trees, sticks, rocks, life aside, wide
enough for our wagons to squeeze through, be hauled up,
which they do   in only   two days.

We are   finally   going to leave the Wasatch Mountains,
descend down this hill.
I'm too tired, sore, dirty, scraped
to even give a care.

Over dinner, Father turns to Mother, says, "I think
we should celebrate. Maybe you should make a pie."

She stares at him for a full beat
before she says,
      "We've had no fruit for days."

What Charles Thinks

Folding blankets beside the wagon,
I smell the familiar scent of tobacco
as Charles appears at my side.
He's usually quiet in the evenings, quiet in the day.
His silent presence is becoming familiar, comfortable, warm.
But tonight the words spill forth, as if they cannot be contained.

"Miss Graves," he says, nods.
I smile. "You know it's Mary Ann."
The beginnings of a laugh reach his mouth
because we've been through this a dozen times.

"I wondered if you would like
to . . . take a walk with me?"

"A walk?" I ask, my worn-out legs flinching as I speak.

He blinks, takes a small step.
"I realize it's almost dark . . . I thought
maybe we could go somewhere . . . to talk . . ."

I try not to laugh at this, point out
we've been side by side for many days,
plenty of time to talk. Instead I try being
silent, tossing him a quilt from the pile,
pick up another one for myself, start to fold.
I look at him and smile.

He ducks his head a little, watching
my hands, then busies his own
folding the quilt I gave him.
"I wanted to tell you
I've enjoyed your company," he says.

I smile at that, genuine, will myself
not to speak—not to wrinkle this moment.
We both place our folded quilts
in the basket. I pick up the last blanket from the other pile.

"I hope," he says, empty hands now nervously
twitching in front of him, "that we can see more
of each other . . . when we arrive in California."

"You're convinced we're going to get there,
are you?" I say, before I remember not to. "Seems like
this journey will never end."

He laughs, drops his hands
to his side, straightens his shoulders.
"Miss Graves," he says, suddenly serious.
"You are the nicest person I've ever known."

   And I can't think
   of what to say
   to that,

so I bend over to stack the empty
baskets at my feet.

"I will search for you on the trail tomorrow," he says.

I hear him walking away
and imagine he's quite pleased.
I stand up, wish there were more blankets to fold.

The nicest person he's ever known.   My God.
Who does he think I am?

Great Salt Lake

John drives the oxen harder than usual,
in a hurry to get away from this place,
away from this group, away from us all.
I watch him wave his whip,
know exactly how he feels.

We spill out
of the mountains, trickle down
to the lake. It sits before us,
wide, calm, enormous,
like it has always been.

Some of the little ones up ahead run
to the edge, but Father stops us, away from the others,
says, "Let's set up camp. Save your strength.
We'll want an early start tomorrow."

A gloom of sour surrounds him,
exhaustion, frustration.
The coffee we just bought is almost gone.
We've caught no fish, killed no game, for days.

We should have reached this lake three weeks ago,
I wonder if it knows.
There's a smell in the air,
like a bad egg broken in the henhouse,
and we are so tired,
too exhausted, beaten down to care
whether this place
is beautiful or not.

Fall

Following Tracks

Early mornings are cool now,
an unwelcome chill
that worry cannot seem to warm.

There is comfort in
the tracks before us — Hastings — that we follow,
impossible to tell how fresh they are
but easy to pretend the wheels that made them
lie just up ahead,
over the hill, around the bend,
a short length away from the end. But then —
                    a note —
weathered into pieces,
clinging to a bush,
appearing as if it's
been here for too long.

Mrs. George Donner kneels
in the middle of a gathering of silence,
brings the pieces of paper together
one by one. We watch, hold
our breath, while she works
this ragged puzzle.

                    "It's Hastings's hand," she says.

                    "Two Days.
                    Two Nights.
                    Hard Driving.
                    Cross Desert.
                    Reach Water."

Her voice cracks
at the end,
already parched.

Packing for the Desert

"Two days is not that bad," Sarah says.
"We'll celebrate the sight of the Humboldt River
when we come out the other side."

We gather
all the grass we can pick, all the water
we can contain, pack it
into the wagons in almost-silence,
as though we are trying to take this place
with us, like
a children's game,
except even the children
are somber,
painted with fear.

Moonlight

We make our way through the cedars,
over the ridges dotted with sagebrush until

before us there's a never-ending whiteness,
thick and cracked, silent.

Long before dusk settles,
we rest. The men say it's better to sleep

now, set out in the cool
of night, as if we're slipping away

while the sun's
turned her back.

It's too hot for sleep, but rest
is always welcome.

I don't remember closing my eyes
but a chill greets me when I open them again. Night.

The moon is not quite
half lit, as if it's trying to hide,

but can't resist peeking around a corner to see
if it's being watched,

so its light escapes,
finds its way down to the ground,

where it's reflected back to us
by the white salt sand — the most beautiful land.

The air is cool. The ground shimmers
below us as if we're great lords and ladies

and the moon has rolled out a carpet of jewels
to announce our arrival. I wonder why the note

didn't mention this at all, why a person would live his whole life,
never get to see this.

All Night

All night we walk without
the sounds that surround
us in daytime or the warmth.
Here is only dark sky, filled with stars, cold air,   us.
The salty ground crunches underneath our feet, a sound
cool, crisp, like the air that surrounds us.

We are quiet, sleepy, walking
forward in a daze, hoping
we're making good time.
The chill around us thickens
as the beauty thins.

Day One

Day breaks,
the sun is welcomed
with her light and warmth.
Everything seems better
for the briefest of moments.
But the glare from the sun on the white ground
is brighter than the moon's,
causing us to narrow our eyes, stumble
to find a place to look. The wind turns up,
hot, harsh, blowing salt in our eyes,
on our faces, dusting my dress white,
the color of old overnight.
The ground below us
sops up the sun faster than we walk,
taking in the heat,
melting something deep.
It bubbles up, cracks the ground at our feet.
The wagon wheels sink deep,
crack the top, get underneath
where it's hot and wet. The wheels
move on, making a sucking, gulping sound,
making a sticky film on the top like melted
caramel on a cake.
Everything sticks.
Skin to clothes, clothes to air.
As if this ground is going to suck us in.
The sun shines too brightly, hotly, boasting
that it had a full night's sleep.

Could a day be any longer?

On and On

On and on
                        we walk,
keeping our direction
                        by watching the sun,
willing it
                        to move faster,
willing us
                        to move faster.

We drink
                        the coolness
as it settles
                        in large gulps,
unafraid now
                        of the coldest night,
we walk on.

Night

The cold
comes faster,
sharper, harsher.
The little ones
want to ride
but Father says,   "We all
        must walk, spare the oxen."
Lovina brings over the quilt,
folds me into it beside her.
Frank tries to come too,
but I'm too tired to trip over him
so I wave him over to Mother, take Eliza
instead who will get heavy in my arms
but warm my chest just the same.

Rest

We don't go far.
Other than a short rest at noon,
no one has slept for two days.
Jonathan and Nancy have been crying softly for a while.
So we stop,
feed and water the beasts,
feed and water ourselves,
tie up things tight, safe.

I've never welcomed sleep
such as this.

Next Day

Father wanted to set out before
light, but dark is gone
when we rise. It's another morning, filled with
sun.
So quiet here, no sounds
of birds chirping, no sounds of grass blowing,
no sounds of trees swaying. No sounds of
life of any kind.
There's only this
one last day and a bit of night
before we reach respite.
Knowing that it ends today
helps me face the sun.

Day Gone

another day

                                   spent

water's almost gone

night

                                   cold

we continue on

walking in our sleep

Sunrise

The sun comes up
       light
shines on what lies ahead
a low bit of land hanging between two hills,
surely it's the end.
I can hold on.

We walk.

Heartbreak

In between the hills, we stand
at the highest point,
we see

              desert

                  more desert

                          I cannot see an end

Day Three

hot sun approaching

but we must rest

no one can go on

we collapse

in the shade of the front of the wagon, knowing

it will soon be gone

Moving Again

Father shakes me awake,
covered in sweat.

"We have to keep going," he says,
his lips cracking open.

I stand, damp and dizzy,
move thickly

behind the wagon for a drink.
Mother is slowly, carefully pouring

water into Frank's mouth,
not a drop is spilled.

She pulls away the jug,
he whines.

Lovina steps up next. Mother moves the jug
around, listening to the swish.

I see the ease she lifts it with,
hear the sounds of scarce,

turn around,
try not to swallow,

Lovina comes too.
"We'll get to water soon," I say.

But then I close my lips
because letting out words,

letting in air, makes my throat
crack with dry.

Day Three Ends

The day melts

into night,

cold and long.

My feet ache to stop

but my mouth aches more

with thirst

so I keep going.

My Lips

The sun,   the heat,   are cracking them

open,   ripping them   apart,   while the wind

blows salt   onto them   to sting.   I think

about speech   but every time   I move them,

I taste   the metal air,   they bleed.

It's easier   to   leave them   be.

More Time Passes

there is cold.

there is heat.

there is rest.

there is axle grease for bleeding lips.

there are metal bits to suck for spit.

there is no wagon train,

only families moving together, passing others by.

there is no help to be given.

there is only forward.

there is no water left.

Others

we pass the Reeds

now on foot   their oxen giving out.

we pass William Eddy

whose children aren't crying

a scary silence that keeps our eyes

pointed straight ahead.

we pass Keseberg, who's lightened his wagon of old man Hardcoop,

who walks slower than everyone else, always in the rear,

now walking so far behind

he looks as if he's alone.

all of them covered in white

dust   as if the desert ground has given them all

ghost faces.

we don't speak.

don't look at them. they don't

look at us.   we just look ahead, search

ahead, keep our eyes forward,

begging for a glimpse of

the end.

Ahead

Ahead   I only see   waves of heat

       curving the land   smearing the sky

       but Will yells, "I see it!"

and he points   and I nod   with the others

because I can't open   my mouth to speak

       because I am sure   there is nothing

    there because   I want   to pretend   he's right

Green

closer we get   and we see trees   green

green from drink

Oh,
it's real

Out

I don't feel the last few steps on white hot salt trying to suck me down my feet glide over it all my eyes don't ever leave the place where there's a creek oh God I see it I keep walking there I'm walking faster so is Frank who is holding my hand the wagon wheels are moving faster the oxen must see it too must smell the water and at some point the ground under me is different not sticky or sandy just soft hard-packed ground my feet don't sink anymore they're lighter and I take those last few steps at a leap wade into the creek feel the water sink into my dress weigh it down and I bend over put my whole face in the water my lips burn but it's a good burn soothing burn my throat tastes

relief

Everyone Else

They stagger in
throughout the day,
one family at a time,
every living thing,
man, woman, child, beast,
goes straight into the water.
We all stay there, by the creek,
in the creek, drinking
until our stomachs make us stop,
and even then we keep cupping the water
up, letting it slide down our faces, our lips,
because it feels so good.
So when night arrives we are mostly wet,
     mostly cold,   mostly happy.

Cold Night

Inventory taken, counting
stops too soon. There is no more sugar,
no more coffee, only a small bit of salt.
The flour cannot be stretched much further than a week.
The meat has dwindled down to small stacks,
small sacks, small piles.
There is not enough
food to last until California. Everyone
falls asleep, cold with fear, cold
with dread.

        We awake to see
the hilltops up ahead have turned, in the night,
to white.   We turn, peer behind us,
over the desert we just crossed, see our path
to safety blocked
by a certain death we've tasted,
its dryness lingering on our lips,
so we turn again,
to the white-topped hills ahead, know there is nothing
now but walking on,
following Hastings's tracks
to the river,
even though
forward is bleak,
ahead is hungry,
onward is unknown.

Someone

Someone
needs to go ahead, ride fast
without strings of wagons, oxen, children,
ride ahead into safety,
bring back some to us.

Bill McCutchen volunteers.
Everyone nods, knows
he will ride fast there, fast
back to his wife and baby girl.
      I glance at Amanda, see her face stretch tight.

But who will accompany him?

"I will," says a voice,
and my lungs cave in.

Charles.

Everyone frowns, passes worry
from eyes to eyes, thinking a bachelor
will have no reason to ride back.

But Charles looks
directly at me and I think
he will return.

What We Leave

Piles of tools,

seven chairs,

a tall framed mirror with only the tiniest of cracks,

heavy books,

heavy trunks,

broken china,

crusted skillets,

a beautifully carved pine bed.

We line them up, neatly, orderly,

an offering to the land.

Hoping for a quicker pace,

we lighten our loads.

Humboldt River

I have never hated water, but this —
the way it curves, glides,
like a sinister smile,
moves so fast
like a taunting child,
dances around the mocking ground,
the very place of land
where we collide with the trail,
the proven route,
the "long way,"
to find the path is cold,
smooth, with time,
the tracks washed away
of those who went right.
No one celebrates
this landmark,
everyone
moves on,
silently seething
at its sight,
our tongues
too full of bitter
to speak.

Days

The days seem

agonizingly long,   frighteningly short.

No will to chatter, pass the time.
No one feels like quilting.

                              The sun rises later, sets earlier,
                              leaving less light in between.

Nothing here to see
in this empty space
of land, only the tumbleweed moves,
blows around in groups and alone,
rootless, nothing keeping them together.
They are at the mercy of the wind.

Sometimes the only sound I hear
while I'm walking is the squeak, cry
of the wagon wheels, whining, *Why,*
    why,   *why.*

John Snyder

He's angry all the time, ready
for his job to be over.
I heard him say to Jay, "I would have gone ahead
for supplies," glaring at Father
before stomping away.

    Amanda says, "I think if he'd gone,
    we wouldn't be seeing him return."

Sometimes John goes
three days without looking at me,
talking to me.   Hard to do
when we're walking
an arm's length apart.
I want to feel annoyed,
but all I can manage is relieved.

The Trail

The men think they're
following a trail, a road
well marked by wheels
and feet, like a street,
pointing you
in the direction you need
to go. But I know.
We follow a trail of broken things
tossed from wagons — family heirlooms
so heavy with memories
the oxen couldn't pull —
quilts, spinning wheels, dishes (too much
dust to see the pattern), wooden bits
once part of something rich,
portraits of great-grandmothers
who'll spend eternity in the desert,
watching beasts pull treasures
while dirty people trail behind. We pass
a rocking chair, the children stop
to sit and rock, one child
at a time, the chair rocks
as we walk, trying not to tread
on the waste, beastly remains,
left behind from those who came
before, left a trail for us to follow,
a trail of crumbs from their lives,
rag dolls, boxes of cutlery, mattresses,
death,   oxen skulls, oxen flesh,
mounds of dirt that will
only blow into the sky, dust
to cover the next caravan until
what's underneath is then on top,
man, woman, or child.

Nerves

Everyone is frayed,
frazzled like a rope
that's come apart,
can't be twined again.

The flour's all gone,
we've had no bread for days.
Now there's only meat,
a few beans, some greens we sometimes find along the way.

The widow Murphy complains about a teamster
paying too much attention to her daughter.
   Her son-in-law whistles so much
   Eleanor says she hears it in her sleep.
      The woman with the dotted dress rolls her head around,
      constantly cracking the bones in her neck.
         "Old man Hardcoop walks too slow . . ."

         "She doesn't think I can hear her . . ."
   ". . . always has to be first . . ."
". . . thinks he's always right . . ."
         ". . . that smell from his clothes . . ."
      ". . . could have sworn I had more flour . . ."
  "He spits all the time . . ."
         "If I have to hear her say, once more . . ."

I cannot wait until we arrive
in California, where I'll never have to think of
these people again.

John

                    I didn't see it,
I was on the other side of the wagon holding Frank's hand
because he was whining, tired, didn't want to move his legs.
The Reed wagon appeared on the left,   so close,   and I heard
John yell,   anger,   heard him crack the whip, thought it was our
oxen he was hitting.   It was not.   Mr. Reed saw
what he was doing, swung down off his horse, ran up to John.
I heard him yell,   "Hey! Stop! You can't beat my oxen!"
heard John yell,   "*Always* trying to be first!"   heard
the whip,   *crack,*   screams,
gasps,   louder than the wheels beside me, I pulled on Frank,
yanked him up where I could see   in that space between
the wagon and the oxen,   so much dust,   hard to see,
Mr. Reed   raising his arms high   swinging at John,
the wagon blocked my view,   I stopped   walking,
I couldn't see,   the wagon passed and   I saw
Mr. Reed standing   still,   knife in his hand,   John
on the ground before him,   crawling,   crawling,
                    crawling,   then
        stop.

They

they yelled He's Bleeding
they yelled Stop the Wagons
they yelled Someone Help
they yelled It's His Chest
they yelled Won't Stop

they gathered around

they clutched their hearts

they got quiet and quiet

they said
              he was dead.

I Didn't Move

I just stood,
      watched it all,
      held on to Frank's hand,
      watched them fuss over John
      then stop.

      No one cried.
      No one was sad.   Everyone
         seemed angry.

Mr. Reed   stood still,
      stepped backward,
      seemed unable to catch his breath.

I Should

I should feel something,
some big hole in my soul
that he's gone.   I should weep or pray
or know what to do with the looks I'm getting
from my family, the almost-pats that glance at my shoulders.
The sound of Eleanor sobbing
makes me squirm.   I want them all
to look away.

> Amanda sidles up beside me, shifts the baby
> on her hip. "You wouldn't have married him
> if he'd asked, right?"   She says it in a spurt,
> like a challenge, as if she already knows
> the answer.

I shake my head.

> "Right," she says. Then she thrusts baby Harriet
> out to me. "Will you hold her
> for a while, then? Take her over to some shade?
> I've got to fill buckets."

I take her baby,
walk away, so grateful for a place to go that I
ignore the fact that Amanda's buckets
are already full.

What to Do

We have to stop, set up camp.
There are decisions to be made.
Mr. Reed stays
in his tent with his family,
friends hovering outside like guards.

Our tent is the center.
Everyone comes, full
of questions and opinions.
        Not about John — no one
        speaks of John.
It's all about Mr. Reed.

"It was murder."   "We should hang him."   "He deserves
a trial."   "I'll stand judge."   "I'll get the rope."
        "His wife and children?"
"Thinks he's above the law."   "He should be dealt with in California."
"Why should we feed and aid a criminal?" "The law says he deserves—"
"There is no law where we are now. This is not governed land."
        "It's murder!"   "Retribution!"
                                        Clunk.
                        Louis Keseberg.
                        Standing before my father,
                        the end of his rifle thumping on the ground.

                        "I will not travel with a murderer.
                        I won't put my wife and children
                        at risk.   He will hang.   Tonight.
                        For taking the life of that Graves boy."

Everyone buzzes an agreement, no one
says, "His name was John Snyder,"
but I'm thinking it so loud and hard
I can't believe they all don't flinch.

Mrs. Reed

sobbing

People clear a path and she enters,
Margaret Reed.
Her face painted with shame, but I wonder if
it's only a layer.
She clasps her hands together
in front of her chest, casts her eyes around,
begs for her husband, begs
for his life to be spared.   She cries
and begs and walks around, looks
in the eyes of every man
until they all look away.

A Compromise

He is banished. That is what they
decide, my father and those men,
looking somewhat relieved,
though I don't know if it's because
they'll soon be rid of Mr. Reed
or because they did not have to kill him.

Only Mr. Keseberg walks away with anger,
his cheeks red, his eyes clear and hot.

John

Mother spends only minutes
stretching out his body, straightening
his clothes.   Sarah moves to wash
his skin, but Mother stops her. "There's no time."

Jay and Father dig a hole, deep
in the ground, praying
it is deep enough to keep
animal scavengers away.

Mother rifles through his pockets, finds a watch,
something to mail to his brother in Illinois.

Everyone in the camp gathers round
as they place him in the ground,
spread dirt over him, cover it with rocks.
Mr. Breen says a prayer.

And that is all.

People walk quickly to where they'll sleep,
speaking of
an early start, a faster pace
tomorrow.

Later I hear Father say
in a worried tone, ". . . one less man to help . . ."
And I hear Mother's answer:
   "One less mouth to feed."

Speed

Everything in the wide plains around us is gentle
and slow, carefree and still. Even the clouds
above us are the drifting kind.
But we move across the land in a pointed line,
straight, determined.
From above, I imagine the birds peer down
at our wagon canvas puffs, surrounded by dust,
think we are clouds on a path,
on our way to a storm.

Time

No one says it,
but the word buzzes
around us unspoken, loud.
                    Hurry.

Women pick up children
who walk too slow.   Men race ahead,
searching for mountain peaks, race back,
on horses, riding beside us
with anxious, twisted
looks, as if they're herding cattle, only
no one stops to graze.
                    Hurry.

Now not only Father counts our heads of cattle.
I see Mother's lips
doing it too.
I know she's thinking
about their meat,
counting how much she has to feed us.
                    Hurry.

Amanda's eyes are always out, scanning the horizon, looking for
the mountains that mean we're almost there,   looking for
Bill, due back any day.
                    Hurry.

Hardcoop

The sun was on its way down
before anyone noticed that
Mr. Hardcoop was no longer walking
among us. There were worried looks
cast over shoulders into the dust,
guilty looks ahead,
everyone hoping he would reappear,
no one stopping or slowing down.

The Fire

When we stop
to camp — the sky already dark —
talk of retracing steps to search for him
flits through the camp like embers spitting from the fire,
moving from one place to the next, quickly
fading out.
The horses are exhausted. Forfeiting
their rest would risk tomorrow's progression.
We can't afford to waste a single tomorrow.
We sit around the fires, shooting hot looks
toward Keseberg for turning out the old man
who'd been riding in his wagon,
shooting hot looks toward Keseberg to rid ourselves of the flames
of shame that burn within us, because none of us
had taken him in.

Jay stands,
begins to cut down extra wood. My father rises
to help. They chop three times as many logs,
build a fire high, high, high. The heat from it sticks
to my dress, burns my skin. All of us stare
at the mountain peak of smoke, hoping
it will lead Hardcoop here, hoping
his legs can bring him on, hoping we'll
have the chance to redeem ourselves, find a place
for him to ride.

Hardcoop

He doesn't come.

We move on.

Days Pass

We walk
    as fast as we can
    from early until late
We walk
    without talk
    of what will happen when our food is gone
We walk
    because in the night Indians
    steal every horse that Father owns
We walk
    because the lighter the wagon,
    the faster the oxen move
We walk
    with only the briefest stop for noon
We walk

We walk

We walk

    haven't seen a mountain yet

Amanda

Amanda lends Father her horse
to use for scouting ahead, puts the supplies
that were on its back in our wagon,
eats from our pot each night.

People eye her during the day,
tell her, "Your husband will be here soon," pretend
to comfort her though they only say it
to comfort themselves.

She's not worried, just
tired.   Tired of holding the baby,
                tired of wearing the same dress, eating
                        the same thing, moving in the same direction.

She wears tired on her face
like a shawl that sags in threads from your shoulders and I know
how she feels.

Nights

There is no gathering round the fire, only slumping
by the wagon, eating the same bowl of soup
too quickly, collapsing
into sleep.
The men still take turns on watch, but not so many now,
as most of the livestock is long gone,
and there's little left to steal.
Our wagon train is shedding wagons,
losing animals, watching people fall away,
like a giant tree whose branches are being chopped off
one at a time, leaving behind
nothing but a skinny stalk.
Lovina picks up the quilt, then puts it back down.
Jay hasn't played his fiddle in days,
but who would have the strength to dance.

I no longer dream
of life in California.
too tired to dream.

Up Ahead

Two men return
from scouting, bring a yell
and news that sends a ripple
of excitement down the wagon train.
Amanda walks straighter, faster, strains
to see what's up ahead. But it's not her husband,
just a view.   Mountains.   We are almost there.

View of the Sierras

Heavy clouds drape
the tops of the mountains, cover up
the tips so that
we cannot see.

A stretch of land
lies rolled out like a fancy rug
between us and them,
the last part of our journey, all laid out ahead.
Simply cross over those peaks
and we will finally have arrived.

The Donners want to stop,
rest the cattle.
But Father says, "We need to keep going,"
his eyes on those clouds.
His voice,   quiet, cold, sure,
leaves me
scared for the first time.

A funny time to be afraid,
right here,

with the end
in sight.

Returned

Early morning brings sun, stretching over
the entire valley, trying to warm the land,
and a trail of dots, approaching in the distance.

People coming.

We stay, circle up our wagons,
while Mr. Donner and his brother ride ahead.

They do not ride back
right away, instead we watch them
     get closer to the dots,
     get off their horses,
     meet on the ground.

We watch them all mount again, ride in
together, getting closer,
closer to us,
     so the dots become horses,
     horses become mules,
     packed heavy with sacks and sacks
     of what can only be food,

          and in the lead, three men on horseback.
          Amanda gives a yelp.

There are two Indians.
And Charles.
Without her husband.

What He Brought

Charles brought
>mules, on loan from Mr. Sutter, packed with
>sacks of flour, a little salt,
>bags of dried meat,
>two Indians, Luis and Salvador, who can help
>>guide us over the mountain peak,
>news that Amanda's husband is alive, but
>>sick, resting up at Sutter's Fort,
>news that Mr. Reed, John's murderer, lives, thin and weak,
>>they'd met him in the mountains,
>>he'd be safe inside by now,

>news that   there was a war on
>>with the Mexicans,
>>there were no men to spare,

>but news that we were close,
>>just a ten-day walk, with winter
>>at least a month away.

>>>Everyone gathers round to hear this news,
>>>everything goes up,
>>>in a circle around him,
>>>our faces lift,
>>>our bodies lift,
>>>our hearts, lift, lift, lift,
>>>as though someone's blown something
>>>underneath us to make us rise:
>>>hope.

Hope

Hope is
the taste of salty sweet
on your tongue, when your teeth
bite into a piece of jerked meat.

Hope is
the sound of children laughing,
adults finding a way to breathe.

Hope is
the feel of a heavy sack, full
of flour, being loaded onto the wagon.

Hope is
the sound of Jay's fiddle,
the sight of people dancing around a fire,
the smell of bread baking in the coals.

Jay's Fiddle

When he plays, couples
stand to dance around the fire.

I watch Sarah's feet tapping,
ankles swaying on the ground where she sits on a log,

watching him.
I start to feel sorry for her, pity,

because she cannot stand up, dance
with her husband,

while his arms are wrapped around
the fiddle,   but then I see

that he looks at her
through every song.

The fast ones, light and fun,
the slow ones, thick with sorrow,

he looks at her as he plays each one,
as if he's telling her something important and big,

as if he's telling her something
private.

You can watch her, watching him, sitting low by the fire,
tapping her feet like an agreeing nod

to whatever it is he's saying,
you can look at her and see

she likes
where she sits.

Staying Put

In the morning there is no talk
of moving on.
It's clear the supplies,
the news, the excitement,
have not yet been digested.

> "We'll rest up
> for a few more days," Mr. Donner says
> at noon. "And then we'll make our cross."

I watch Father's face to see what he thinks
of this plan.
> He twitches.
> He frowns.

One Thing After Another

One day brings a death.
One of the widow Murphy's sons-in-law,
cleaning a gun, accidentally shoots another.
There's a day of cleaning, praying, burying.
And then another day
which brings an injury to Mr. Donner's hand,
a gash wide and deep, received
while he was repairing a wagon wheel.
Women bring herbs, balms, the last of whatever they have,
which isn't much.   A day of rest passes.

Father's anxious now, stirring around like a storm,
spreads the seed of "push on through"
"weather's coming"   "rest when we arrive."
Some men follow him along. Others
shrug it off, tell him Donner needs more time.

It's no surprise when Father announces
we're leaving.   We're going on ahead.
Others are coming with us. The Breens, the Reeds,
Charles.

> Mr. Donner says, "Go on.
> We'll catch up with you
> in a few days' time,
> see you in California."

And so our party splits.

Truckee Lake

It rains all day as we cross the valley, a cold rain
that stops at sunset, just as we've crossed the golden rug, arrived
at the end of flat
where a cabin stands, roughly made, from travelers in the past.
I see why they lingered. I almost wish we could.

The lake spreads before us, capturing the pines
around the edge that grow up, the mountains in front of us
that point up, taking them, pointing them down
in the image on the surface of the lake, like a sign
that has fallen, as though there is no up or down, as though
there is only here.

The lake is so beautiful, the sky
so clear, wide, clean, full of colors,
when the night arrives,
I hear men talking about the ring around the moon, saying it's a sign
that a storm's coming.   But I stare up at the moon, think
only beauty lies ahead.

During the Night

The Donners didn't come,
but up ahead, on the mountain,
in the sky over our camp,
under the moon,

the snow did.

Morning

Yesterday's rain has changed
into today's snow.

It's not any colder, the snow, easier
than rain — softer, drier, lovelier.

      But Father is terrified.

It's simply a little snow,
                     soft,
                              harmless,

but he hurries us about, snaps at Will
when a cow temporarily escapes.

So we all move, pack, begin
as quickly as we can.

Up

Up we go, in the snow,
leaving the lake behind.
It does not take much
distance up the mountain and suddenly

the oxen breathe out white puffs of worry,

the air is thick with cold,

the ground is thick with snow

that my feet feel through the holes in my shoes

until my skin goes numb.

Everything's being slowly painted white,

as if we're climbing up into winter.

Soon it stills the trees.

Soon the grass is gone.

Soon I cannot see the path.

The Wind

The wind will not stop
breathing down hard upon us,
trying to push us aside,
push us back down the mountain
with its cutting breath.
It breathes right through
my dress — once too stiff,
thick for summer's heat — now
too thin, not enough.

It roars and moans,
picks up snow from the ground,
spits it in my face,
trying to get our attention,
but we tuck down our chins,
squeeze tight our eyes,
vow it will not be heard.

The Snow Thickens

The snow thickens,
covers the trail, hides it away
like a secret.

We stop, not to rest, but because it's clear
the wagons can't go on.
There's a shuffling of goods
being pulled from the wagons.

"Should I bring the fabric?"   "Hand me the tobacco."
    "As much of the flour as we can carry."   "... Mama's quilt ..."
        "... the Bible ..."   "I can't leave that behind."

Busily we pull out things,
wrap them up in blankets, strap them
on the backs of cattle
who aren't used to hauling this way,
aren't relieved to be untied,
aren't cooperating at all.

"Quickly now!"   "That's enough."
        "We've got to press ahead."
    "Just one more look."
                "One more thing."

Around us, the snow thickens.

Mother has me and Lovina stand like a wall
beside the wagon while Father pulls out the wooden plank
with the coins — careful
that no one else will see — and wraps them in a cloth,
hangs it around her neck.

The sun is on its way down
as we move again up, leaving our wagons behind.

The men have their hands full,
        keeping the cattle moving, keeping them together.
We women have our hands full too—
carrying the little ones whose legs
aren't long enough to step up, over now.
My arms ache from Frank's weight, my legs burn with exhaustion.

". . . just a little farther . . ."   ". . . almost there . . ."
                "California's on the other side . . ."

Around us, the snow thickens.

The Longest Day

Early this morning
   cold
       we tried to rush
      everyone
  frantic
     up the mountain
    wishing we could scurry
      like chipmunks
but five feet of snow
      covering the land
        above us
         wagon wheels slipped
     we couldn't walk
       steep
         rocky
      despair
    crazy
        frantic
     mules fell into snow
   Now   Indians cannot find the road
oh, God
   five feet
      the little ones cannot even see
 and my arms oh, God my arms
      ache from carrying them
   none of us can go on
 we stop
       just stop
    and huddle together
   on the side of the mountain
     and darkness falls down on us
   and sleet
and snow

Night

Jay made a fire
on the side of the mountain
in the snow
set a whole tree up in flames
oh, it is so warm
that even though Charles is talking,
telling us all we need to get up   move
we need to cross the pass tonight
before any more snow comes,
I know he has no words strong enough to pull us
up onto our feet   pull us away from this fire
we all sit as close as we dare
Sarah keeps telling
the little ones
it will all be fine,
that in the morning light,
this won't seem quite so bad,
that tomorrow we'll get through
she peeks over at Father
but the snow keeps coming
landing on his beard
so I can't see his face to know
if he agrees
but I can see one of the Indian guides, Luis,
standing under a tree
a blanket wrapped around him
his face so smooth
I can see

he thinks

we are doomed

Winter

The Next Morning

It is thickly silent,

when I feel myself

coming awake.

I am so tired and sore

unsurprised when the blanket feels heavy

as I move a little,

unwrap myself.

I stand,

shake the snow

from my blanket,

it falls without a sound,

the hush of snow on snow.

There is nothing to be heard.

There is nothing to be seen — only white.

We've been buried alive.

My feet stay still

but I turn at the waist,

look around, take it all in.

I can't breathe.

I can't speak.

I hear an exhale behind me and swivel.

Father.

He doesn't see me

but I see him,

his face twisted

in pain, anger, resentment, fear.

Someone calls from somewhere close.

A shout.

A cry.

A shock.

Around me   the ground moves,
                    mounds shift,
            snow erupts   and crumbles
        as one by one
they emerge from the snow,
            pop up from the white,
                        like flowers coming alive
            only to find
    it wasn't spring.

Back Down

What else can we do

but dig ourselves out

 and slowly,

  slowly

   make our way

    back

    down.

The Descent

How strange,
after all this moving west,
to turn around, now, here
with the end in sight,
walk in the wrong direction.
No one says much.
Even the animals are silent.
Along the way, we meet our wagons,
abandoned, alone,
covered in snow.
We stop to dust them off,
fill them again, tether the cattle
back in their yokes.

Frank is in my arms,
the snow higher than his waist.
He asks me, "Why
are we going back down?"
Behind me a wagon wheel creaks, someone
lets out a tiny sob.

At the Lake

The men decide

here we will make a temporary shelter,

here we will set up a temporary camp,

here we will wait — only a few days —

for the snow to melt.

The Camp

The Murphys use
one side of a giant rock
as the wall for their shelter.
Mr. Eddy bargains for some tools.
Mr. Keseberg argues with Mr. Breen,
who has started unpacking some things
in the cabin that already stood.

The teamsters are quick to jump in,
help haul trees,
for the promise of a space to sleep,
a share of meat.

A man they call Dutch Charley returns from scouting,
tells us the Donners are camped at a creek,
a half day's walk away.

I find Amanda, tell her, "Come on.
There's room for you with us."

Father moves away from all this,
away from the lake, so much space
between the others and the place
where he starts our shelter, it's as though we
aren't a part of the camp at all.

Building a House

There are plenty of logs, plenty of space,
any piece of ground we want,
any tree we please.

When the men chop one down
to use as food for the fire,
                                    it falls,
        sinks,
                the snow swallows it whole,
        impossible to find
                        unless you saw it land.

By the day's end,
the trees are felled, logs cut, carried,
notched at the ends, laid together like a puzzle,
while the hides of the oxen are laid over the rafters,
a draped roof.
We make this shelter, this double-sided cabin, our temporary
home. Two doorways left open to let in the light. One side
for us. The other side for
Mrs. Reed and her children. She'll take in
some teamsters, the Indians, and Charles.

    Skins
for a roof,
        skins tied to corners,
        skins stretched tight
above us.
Every time the wind blows,
they flap and bleat in answer.

Unpacking

The others are pulling out a few blankets from their wagons, a bit
of food, an extra piece of clothing or two.

> Father says, "Unpack it all.
> Take everything out of the wagon."

Mother doesn't even flinch,
sets to work right away.

> Will says, "But won't we have to repack it
> all in a few days when the snow melts?"

> Father stares at him
> for the longest time,
> gives his head the slightest shake.

Next to me, Harriet starts to cry
on Amanda's hip. Amanda turns
to face me, says, "Your father
knows about mountain snow."

She says it like a statement,
but in her eyes, there's a question.
Maybe a tiny shred of hope.
I nod, watch it
go away.

Days Pass

It snows.

Everyone is busy,
dismantling wagons, sealing up a shelter,
counting provisions, tucking them away.
I watch Mother take the coins
from their secret place around her neck,
tuck them underneath the mattress that's been carried inside.
I watch her take the last chunk of loaf sugar,
small bits of dried meat, a sack of beans,
put them up on the wooden plank that Jay nailed inside,
perched there in plain sight,
with everyone's eyes on guard.

Outside the cabin,
it snows.

The Cattle

There was nowhere to put the cattle, nowhere
to keep them out of the snow,
nowhere they could walk, graze, find food,
no way to feed them, prevent them
from being buried alive.
They are all dead.
Father and Will slaughtered them
one by one. Jay cut away their skins,
laid them out to dry, hacked apart
their bones, their flesh,
handed it in chunks to Sarah, Eleanor, me.
We carried them, flesh pressed
against our chests,
to the side of a tree, buried them in the snow.
Eleanor worries aloud the snow will melt, spoil our food.
Sarah counts, measures, keeps her worry inside.
I scrub the red
from my hands with snow, turn it pink,
peer down at my dress,
scarlet stain on my chest,
that will never fade.
This dress cannot be saved.
I think about the cattle, how
they carried our things, kept us going, how
slowly they moved, kept us from going, how
many times we stopped because they
had to rest, how, when the snow was falling on the mountain,
Charles and the Indians went ahead, without any oxen,
could have crossed, but we
did not abandon these beasts, our things. We stayed behind
with them. Now they
are all we have left
unless help arrives.

Waiting

There is not much to do now.
The shelters are built,
supplies have been sorted.
So now we sit,
wait,
will the snow to go.

Lovina, Sarah, and I are on a mattress,
the quilt spread out over our laps,
adding another layer of warmth. We stitch
slowly, slowly, slowly,
as if to make the task in front of us last
as long as it possibly can.

Help

Outside people stand in clumps,
watch the snow, watch the sky.

I am inches away from Mrs. Reed when she
says, "We can't get across.

We'll run out of food.
We're going to die here.

We are." And I'm inches away from Charles
when he turns to her and says, "Help will arrive,

Mrs. Reed. Don't worry.
Mr. Reed will come."

I remember what he said down in the valley
about the war, the men being all gone.

I remember how he described Mr. Reed,
Amanda's husband too,   tired,

sick, weak.   I see his face right now
as he's assuring this woman and

I think
he's wrong.

Father

People come to our
cabin, ask Father about
the weather and how to get over
the mountain. They know he grew up in Vermont,
where the winters are harshly thick.   He answers their
questions, shares his wisdom, but keeps
his strength here with us.

Animals

Eddy killed a bear.
So heavy he had to ask Father for help
dragging it to camp, then had to share the meat.
It was alive with flavor on my tongue,
after weeks of beef that had none.

But it is gone.

He goes out every day with his gun, sometimes
returns with a squirrel or a young
coyote or something else so small he can carry it in one hand.
There are so few things that run, walk, climb.

But there are birds.
I see them land in the trees, take flight
again, fly away to wherever they want.

The Lake

Will, Lovina, and I go to the lake.

Will has tied a hook
to the end of a found string.
He pierces a small chunk of liver
from a cow onto its end.

The lake's edge is ringed with ice,
too thin to stand upon,
so he goes as close as he can to the water,
throws it as far out as he can.

It lands with a lonely plop.
And we wait.
                    We see no movement in the lake.
          We wait in the cold wind,
                    on the cold ground,
          we wait.

                    Will drags in the string,
                    moves on down the bank,
               throws it in again . . .
          we wait
                         . . . several times.
                              We do not speak.

               Sometimes when he brings in the string,
                              the meat is gone.
                    Once we watch it arc off in the air,
                              as he casts his line.
And we wait
          until the bits of liver are gone,
               until we decide to go home,
                    fishless, cold.

Melting

It's been four days of sun,
bright clear skies.
I haven't felt warmth
but some must have been delivered.
The trees that were felled at snow level
are now rising up
from the snow line.

Frank asks if the stumps are growing.

Will says, "Stumps don't grow.
Only trees can grow. These aren't trees anymore;
they're stumps. They can't grow."

I kneel down in front of Frank,
look right into his eyes, say, "The snow melting
is a good sign." I pat his shoulder,
hand him a bucket. "Now go fill up
this pail with clean snow,
take it inside to Mother."

Frank moves away, eager to help.

Sarah places her hand on my shoulder,
as I'd done with Frank.
"The snow's melting, Mary Ann," she says, slowly
savoring every word. "Only a few more days of this
and it will be clear enough to cross."

The Next Day

There is no sun.

Only snow.

More snow.

More snow.

Escape

Charles comes by,
    the twinkle in his eye,
    the sleekness of his dress,
gone.

    He tells Father he's returning the mules to Sutter,
        lead a few of the men across,
    bring back more supplies.

"Then we'll all go," I say,
and all the heads turn to me,
where my hand has stopped sewing,
holding the needle up above the quilt,
frozen in midair.

    Charles frowns and looks away,
                Father clears his throat,
                shakes his head, turns to Charles.
                "Good luck to you, then," says Father.
I watch a sag of disappointment
drip down Charles's face.
His eyes look like he wants to say something,
but he doesn't even open his mouth.

From across the room, Will calls out, "I'll go."
Charles looks from Will to Father. He nods his head,
but it's apparent as I watch him glance at Father
that he did not hook his prize.

Will

Will brings in extra wood, helping us
get ready before
he leaves.   He sees me watching
him, tells me later in a voice
low and cold, "We're running
out of food. I can't stay here."

I know he's right. But setting out
in the snow when you cannot see a path
seems almost just as bad.

Will asks Amanda, "Do you want
to send something to Mr. McCutchen? I can take him
something, if you want me to."

Amanda eyes Will for a moment,
                            as though he's crazy,
searches around the room, bare and cold,
where we all sit, trying to stay warm.

                    "Tell him to hurry."

Layers

I shiver
inside layers and layers of cloth,
another dress on top of my travel green, now colorless with grime,
a shawl, a blanket wrapped around at all times,
gloves, scarf, a rag around my face,
sleeves tied at my wrists,
petticoats tied at my ankles,
anything to keep heat from escaping.

"You're the belle of the ball, Mary Ann,"
Eleanor says. I frown, until I see
she's got a teasing smile.

"It's the latest fashion," I say.
Then I help her bundle, tie, mimic my style.
We both twirl about, make the others laugh.

Outside of me grows larger,
layers and layers of cloth,
piled onto each other,
but I'm afraid there's
nothing left
underneath.

They're Back

Like a ghost,
Will comes through our doorway,
cold, hobbling,
waking us all from sleep.
Eleanor gasps. Lovina gives a weak scream.
Mother is up, out of bed, pulling off
his snow-covered wrap, as if his appearance is
nothing unexpected.
He shivers, shakes with exhaustion.
I clamp down on a dozen questions
that sear the end of my tongue.
Father moves to take over for Mother,
peeling off wet layers, checking for frostbite,
while Mother puts the pot back on the fire,
as if she thinks heat will make the food reappear.

"Stanton made us turn back," Will says. He looks at me with anger.
His voice cracks into the room
like a tree limb snapping from the weight of ice.
"We got to a place where the snow was taller than the mules,
they couldn't get through. But Stanton wouldn't leave them.
He turned around, came back.
Said he'd promised Sutter he'd return the donkeys.
Wasn't going to show up without them."

Mother's back stiffens
by the pot she is stirring.
Will shrugs his shoulders, tilts his head.
I cannot tell if he's frustrated or relieved.
Father shakes out the blanket he holds,
snow falls in clumps onto the ground.
He does not say a word, but I look at his hands, see
his knuckles are white.

Words

The next day, I'm outside with Jay
and Father, helping them carry in
wood for the fire, when Charles appears.
            "Would you like some help, Miss Graves?" he asks.
I turn to him, see
his clothes are dirtier, his beard is now untrimmed,
he doesn't have his pipe.
            "Mules, huh?" Father says.
            His words are sharp and loaded.
                        Charles turns to face him, though he doesn't
                        say a word.
            Father passes a log to Jay, keeps his eyes on Charles.
            "Will tells me you turned around because of the mules?"
                        Charles does not flinch. He nods his head
                        solemnly, keeps his eyes on Father as if
                        he's not ashamed.
                        "I made a promise, sir. Mr. Sutter is expecting
                        me back with them; I gave my word.
                        I am a man of my word."
                        His words are without defense, malice, or anger.
                        They're formed simply, said
                        simply, passed to my father plain and true.

"You're a fool," Father says.
"A starving fool."
He passes me the ax, picks up the last
two logs, walks toward the cabin.
"We'll see how you feel about your word when
all our food is gone."

The Quilt

It's finished.

We've nothing left

to sew.

Cough

Baby Harriet has
a cough — small, constant. She sleeps more than
she should.
Amanda asks Mother what to do,
Mother says, "Vinegar
would be good,"   but it's all gone,
no one has any at all.

So they get some snow, boil it
all day, boil it down until it's just a bit of water,
hoping it will become stronger,   powerful,
so they can make her drink some once it cools.

We all spend the day
watching
   the water
   boil away.

Jay's Fiddle

Mother put Jay's fiddle on the shelf
with the food,
but Jay hasn't played.

This morning is so heavy that Sarah
sighs loudly, crosses the room, picks it up,
brings it to her chin.   Everyone sits up
straighter, draws in a breath,
because here is something new.
Sarah looks at Jay, slumped on a mattress, leaning
against the wall,
then she brings up the bow to the side,
tilts her head just so.   "Is this right?" she asks.
Jay's head moves off the wall a fraction of an inch,
one corner of his mouth rises up, an almost-smile.

Sarah pushes the bow across the string. Sound
fills the room.
Harriet stops her tiny cry.

Then Sarah pushes the bow to her neck, pulls it away
again, fast and quick, over and over, her arms moving
like Jay's do on a fast jig,
                but the sound
is a calf that can't find its mother, bleating in worry.

She goes on like that, the fiddle screeching
in a way that makes my neck coil into my shoulder,
a shudder like I've eaten a too-green apple.

Jay is up, crossing the room. He takes the bow
and fiddle from her hands so quickly
the sound stops as if it ran out of air.
Sarah stands there, her arms still up by her shoulders, her hands
empty, her mouth slightly open.

Jay laughs.
A warm chuckle that grows
to a loud breath-sucking chortle,
as much of a shock to the air in this cabin
as Sarah's music had been.

I watch my sister lower her hands
onto Jay's arms, and she is laughing too.
Nancy giggles beside me. Frank covers his ears,
says, "It's not supposed to sound like that!"
which makes everyone laugh even harder,
even Will.

It wasn't music.
But it was something.

More Snow

This morning
the snow on the ground
around the doorway of our cabin
stands six inches taller than it did last night,
as if it arrived when our backs were turned,
covered up our tracks,
all signs that we are here.

The Mules

Jay says he heard the mules
were gone, run off,
or maybe buried alive.

"No one's seen any sign of them.
Stanton's all torn up."

I dart my eyes around the room,
take in all the others.

Sarah, lips tight, head tucked down,
Amanda shaking her head,

Mother closing her eyes.

Will says, "Well, that figures,"
his voice bitterly thick.

Father is silent,
but I can tell
his thoughts are sharp.

My Hair

I have freed it from braids and it hangs
now, loose tangled coils that reach down
the middle of my back.
Mother saw me doing it. "Don't," she said.
"You'll get lice."
But my scalp already itches,
my body feels like I've another
layer of skin, a hide of grime, dust,
dirt, sweat. The hems of this dress, my sleeves,
have gone from dirty gray to deathly black,
a color I will never be able to scrub away.

And it's warmer with my hair down.

Eating

I want to eat slowly,
   make it last,
chew and chew
   until my mouth doesn't want
to chew again,
   let each bite spend time
on my tongue
   so the flavor might be found.
But I can't stand to watch Frank
   finish his bowl, glance around, hungry,
see there's some still in mine.
   So I eat it up fast,
eat it up completely,
   leave nothing behind
but shame.

A Hole in the Ice

Will and I go back to the lake.
The ice around the edge, thick now,
a floor we can walk upon.
Will takes the saw, cuts away
a hole wide enough we can sit down beside it,
drop in our line,
wait for the fish.
They come from all directions,
slowly moving through our view,
a fin here,
    twist there,
        glimpse of big, blank eyes.
At first I hold my breath
each time I see a shape, but soon
I forget not to breathe
because our line never pulls, the fish never nibble.
They never stop to bite.
Sometimes Will pulls up the line
to see if the hook is empty,
but the beef is always there.
We sit
until the cold rings my ears, cuts
into my toes, and Will says, "Let's go."
But I say, "Wait."
And then I lean forward, over the hole,
peer into the water and wait . . .
        wait . . .   wait . . .
               my hands out stiff in front of me
until I plunge them
toward the dark shape darting below,
plunge them into icy wetness,
pull them up holding
nothing but cold.

Charles

I walk away from the lake,
another failed attempt,
cold, empty, numb.
I'm almost home when I see him
coming out of the other side of our cabin — Charles.
We both stop our steps, look up at each other.
There's a blanket wrapped around him,
taking away all shape.
From the neck down he could be a quilt, hanging limply
on the line on a breezeless day.
His face is like a shriveled bulb, pulled up from the soil.
His eyes, still kind, do not reflect
back to me what I know he must see when he looks my way,
the eyes of a gentleman, always filled with polite.

> "Miss Graves," he says,
> looking away. He moves
> to take a step. But I stop him.

"I was at the lake," I say,
holding up the string and hook.

> His eyes take in the shriveled bit of beef,
> then quickly dart away.

And something worse than hunger settles in my gut.

It's my turn to look away.

> He clears his throat, takes a step,
> continues on his path.
> "Good day, Miss Graves," he says,
> as he walks off in the snow.

Conversation with Mother

She's standing over the soup,
Eliza sitting on our new quilt at her feet,
everyone else sent out to swallow
fresh air.

"We should share some food with Mr. Stanton."

As if she doesn't hear me, she keeps her back to me,
stirs the pot.   "Did you catch anything?"

"He brought back all that food."

She turns at the waist, peers at me
over her shoulder. "Shake off the blanket outside,
Mary Ann. You're making it colder in here."

"He's thin, Mother. Way too
thin. Did you see
how weak he looked?"

"Everyone is weak.
Everyone is thin."
She's turned around again, giving me her back.

"But he . . . he doesn't have
a family . . . didn't have a wagon . . .
didn't have any supplies or meat of his own."

Eliza whines now, a weak
cry like she wants to be picked up,
though she doesn't raise her arms.

"Mother, he came back.
He went all the way to safety
and came back. Brought us all food."

Eliza cries. But it's easy
to talk over her sound.

"You never turned away people
at home. Never. We always shared
whatever we had."

She whips around,
her whole body.
"This is different, Mary Ann.
I can't watch my children starve
as I take some of our food,
give it to some stranger."
She bends over, picks up Eliza,
whose tiny body
arches away from Mother's
as if she finds no comfort there.

I've never seen her look this mean,
never seen her this afraid.

Snow

At home   snow meant   extra layers for walking to the barn,
extra quilts on the beds,
extra logs brought in to dry before
    they found their crackle in the fire.
At home   snow meant   snow cream made with milk and sugar,
sliding down a hill on wooden boards,
time inside,
more sewing, more mending, more stories.
At home   snow meant   more time, more work, more layers,
    all to reach the barn,
    feed the animals each day.

Here   snow means   snow
snow means   covered
snow means   silence
snow means   stuck
snow means   trapped
snow means   starving.

Here   it's as if we're   the animals   in the barn,
the snow is too big,   too wide,   too much,
and no one   is coming   to feed us.

Soon the blanket of white
will cover us completely.

In the spring, when people cross
through this land,

with the blanket gone,
what will they find underneath?

Fish

In the cabin, everyone leans
up against the wood, on the bed,
against each other. The skins
overhead sag with the weight of the snow.
No one moves much;
no one says much.
There is only sitting,
waiting,   leaning.

Every day Mother says, "You should try again
at the lake."   And each time, Will and I
look at each other, say nothing,
because we know
the fish won't eat what's left of our beef,
and it's too cold to fail.

Bones

Mother is determined that the meat
left not be used.
She guards it,
moves it
from place to place, so it cannot be
found.   She cooks instead with bones,
picked clean of meat,
boiled through of flavor.
She cooks some again, again, until
they collapse from the inside,
get absorbed into the boiling snow,
fill the pot with a paste,
gray,   thick,   full of nothing,
that she makes us eat even though our tongues
recoil.

The Camp

People stay inside now,
not much moving
about. No one bothers
standing on the slope, searching for
help.   Father ventures out sometimes, brings back
news.

   News of sick babies, coughing women, weakened men.
   News of food dwindling, spirits diminishing, growing desperation.
   News that a teamster for the Reeds, the albino one, has died.

Down at the other camp, Mr. Donner's hand
has not healed,
he no longer leaves his bed.

I hear this news,
take it all in,
look around the cabin,
at these people, this large lot,
my family.
I put my eyes on Frank,
asleep under the finished quilt,
think how much easier it might be
to die alone.

Talk

I hear Mother whispering to Father,
a detailed list of what is left to eat.
It is so precise.
Like a finely carved tray, carefully arranged with crumbs.
I hear her voice shake with a worry
that she does not allow in during the day.
I hear her breath catch when she says Frank's name.
Father doesn't speak for a while,
but when he does, his voice is low and clear,
I catch every word.

"We're all going to die unless someone
gets over that mountain to send for help."

Nothing else is said.
Nothing needs to be.
Even I know
that the only person
who has a chance
of getting over that mountain
is my father.

Yokes

Father sends Will to dig up all the yokes he can find.
Though he knows where he put them,
it takes Will all day to find four.

He brings them in, sets them by the fire.
We watch them, will them to thaw.

Father visited everyone at camp.

> He told them he is crossing,
> it has to be done,
> invited anyone to come.

> He told them they'll need special shoes
> to keep them above the snow, walk without
> sinking down.

> He told them he'll make shoes for anyone who wants to go,
> anyone who knows
> there is no turning back.

After Father's home, our own yokes have been cracked free
of snow and ice,

people start coming to our cabin,
bringing yokes, leather shoestrings,
somber faces.

They don't say much,
they don't stay long.

Father gets up each time,
takes their yokes, puts them with the pile of ours,
sends them out into the cold.

Who Will Go?

Each time the light gets blocked in our doorway, the names blow in.

William Eddy will go,
his wife, children will stay.

William and Charlotte Foster will go,
their son will stay.

Frances, Charlotte's sister, newly widowed, will go,
her daughters will stay.

Their brothers, Lem and Billy, will go,
only 12 and 10,
young enough to not be as useful
as their older brother, John, who must stay
behind
to chop wood for the fire.

Antonio,
Dutch Charley,
hired hands,
Patrick Dolan,
no wife and children,
Salvador,
Luis,
the Indian guides.

We watch them
blow in,
slip out.
We look around
at each other, still and quiet
like creatures in a cage.

Amanda
    holds her baby
    so tight,
    looks at Mother,
    that I know   she will go.

    I am too far away from
Sarah and Jay
    to hear more than
    a scattering of words in quiet voices,
    see them clutch their hands
    together,
    but I see Jay rise,
    talk to Father,
    who nods.
    I see Sarah's eyes
    fill up with fear.

I'm Going

I tell Father
I want to go.
He nods,
does not look up
from the wooden ring
he is pushing out
from the plank
propped between his legs.
Mother nods too, as if
they both expected this.

Sarah's face
appears relieved I'm going with her, Eleanor's
eyes get big with fright,
Lovina and Nancy simply stare.

I do not look at Will.

Frank clings
to my legs, says,
"I want to go with Mary Ann."

I pat him on the head
and then I look away.

Charles Stanton

The next morning he enters
the cabin, holding a yoke.

"Mr. Graves," he says.

Father's eyes flick up from the leather strings
he is wrapping around the wooden ring,
his face draws tight.

Charles's face is thinner than when I saw him last,
the skin hangs a little from his eyes,
like a shadow of the blanket draped around his shoulder.
But his voice is still regal,
his words still carefully carved.

He draws in a breath.
"I've gotten a yoke from the Kesebergs,"
he says, his eyes on Father.
"I'd like to come with you, sir . . .
if that would be all right."

I feel eyes on me,
Nancy's, Eleanor's, Sarah's.
I keep mine on Father,
who says,   "We aren't
turning back."

Charles lowers his shoulders
a little, keeps his eyes on Father.
"I know, sir," he says.
He clears his throat.

Father stares a moment,
takes in the sight of him,
knotted hair, tattered blanket,

hollowed cheeks.
Then he nods,
puts his eyes on his work.

        Charles draws the blanket
        around him tighter, looks over the room.
        Mother looks away. Jay stands, crosses
        to shake his hand.

                "It will be good, Mr. Stanton,"
                Sarah says. "To have someone with us
                who's crossed the pass before."

     "You're going, then, Mrs. Fosdick?" he asks,
     concern on his face.

                "Yes," Sarah says. "Jay and I,
                Father, Mrs. McCutchen, and
                Mary Ann."

     His eyes open,
     darts a look of worry to me.

I hold his gaze,
my face smooth as a rock.

     "Well," he says.
     "Until tomorrow, then."

     And he turns around, adjusts his blanket,
     walks back out to the snow.

Will

He glares at me,
burning cold eyes,
thinking it isn't fair.

That Father,
  his knowledge of snow and mountains,
is going.

That Sarah and Jay,
  no mouths to feed, no reason to stay,
are going.

That I,
  no husband, no babies, too female to chop wood,
am going.

That he,
  the only one strong enough to bring in wood for Mother,
must stay.

We lock eyes,
share a thought.

    It's almost certain   I will die
    out there,   lost, cold, starving,
    on the side of a mountain.

But we both know
  that staying here is worse.

Good-bye

Mother gives Father a chunk of frozen meat,
wrapped in a sack, rounder than Frank's head.
I wonder where it's been all this time.
I do the math, realize
how it must stretch out over seven days.

Amanda presses Harriet tight
against her chest, breathes in her head,
sobs. Mother takes the baby.
Amanda looks away.

> Frank takes the quilt off his side of the mattress,
>   the new quilt,
>   the journey-to-California quilt,
>   brings it to me, dragging it
>   across the ground.
> "Here, Mary Ann," he says.
> "You should take this with you."

I am still for a moment
before I reach down, take the quilt
from his hands, slowly fold it,
giving my throat time to open up again.

"Thanks, Frank," I say.
"But I don't want to get it dirty.
You keep it safe here.
I'll get it when we return."

Eleanor doesn't tell me good-bye,
but last night, in the bed, she took my hand in hers,
gave it a wordless squeeze.

The First Day

It is hard walking away
from camp, walking up the mountain, walking
on top of the snow, climbing in the cold,
with muscles, slight enough to only cling to bones,
    hard to breathe
the air so cold it cuts into my nose,
bites down my throat, slices my lungs,
    hard to follow
the person in front of me,
trudge in a line up the slope,
    hard to think
the last time my feet were here
they walked directly on ground now buried under
snow so thick and packed I can't be sure where it is,
    hard to think that then,
with the ground right there, my footing sure,
with three meals a day inside my body,
I'd thought I was tired, too weak to go on.
            I did not know Tired.
            I had not met Weak.
It's hard to remember
how slowly we moved, bringing so many things
over the mountain, how we'd turned around because of the cattle.
Because of the cattle.
It's hard to think about these things,
so I won't. I turn instead, take a last peek
behind me, down the mountain, a glimpse
back at the camp. But I cannot find it.
There are trees.
There is the lake.
There is white.
But no camp can be seen.
As if there's no one there.

Walking

The day
ticks away
slowly,   slowly,
like our steps
up the side of a mountain
that I cannot even feel,
a mountain covered
in snow so thick and high
there are special shoes on my feet
so I will not sink.
These shoes,
so long,   so heavy,   so wide,
cause my steps   to stretch
farther apart than they are used to doing.
My hips already burn.
I push as much weight as I can
into each of the two
sticks I grip by my sides, like extra limbs,
as though I'm pushing myself up the mountains,
crawling more than walking,
hobbling,
one step at a time.

Keeping Up

Father said no turning back,
but without a yoke to make snowshoes,
Dutch Charley can't keep up. He sinks into each step,
takes twice as long
to come up, twice as long to move ahead.

> Lem and little Billy
> are no better, one pair between them,
> their mother sent them on, thinking
> they'd be light enough to stay on top
> of the snow.   But only a bird could be that light,
> with hollow bones.

> They've taken turns with the snowshoes, but it's
> no use. Charlotte and Frances are pulling them along.

> > "We cannot stop walking
> > while others catch up," Father says
> > into the fire. "Everyone must move
> > as fast as he can. If we wait for stragglers,
> > none of us will make it."

Dutch Charley appears too exhausted, too weak,
to even care what he hears. He collapses in a heap
by the fire, as if he will never move again.

> Lem is panting, worried,
> huddled close to Billy, who seems
> almost frozen with fear.
> Their sisters' faces twist
> with the knowledge that the boys
> won't make tomorrow's fire
> at the rate of today.

Father and Jay leave to gather wood.
Frances and Charlotte clutch
each other's hands, pass whispers back and forth.

I lock eyes
with Amanda. We both say
nothing,   just stare.

This is how I fall asleep.

Turning Back

The next morning Father shakes me awake.
I rise, stiff, every part of me
screaming.

The fire is mostly gone,
everything around me is bitter, brittle,
hard. I sit up, suck in cold air, try to fill my body.

"Mr. Graves," Dutch Charley says.
He's standing, to the side of the fire,
Frances and Charlotte behind him.

"I'm headed back to camp," he says
rigidly, quickly.   "I'm taking one of the boys."
Frances, Charlotte, William Foster stand side by side,
William's face fierce, tense,
bracing for a storm.
Behind them I see Lem and Billy,
each holding one shoe,
unsure where to look, what to do.

I stand up, move toward Father,
but he turns his back, already walking away.

"Fine," he says. "Everyone else,
we leave in three minutes."

The sisters blink in surprise,
but the brothers lock eyes.
I don't want to watch this
but I cannot look away.

        "I'm going where Lem goes," Billy says,
        moving closer to his brother. "Please, Frances.
        I want to—"

But Lem moves in
between Frances and Billy.
"No, Billy," he says, his voice stern,
firm like a father's.
"You're going back to help Mama."
He moves to take the shoe.

          "No!" Billy says, pulling it
          closer to his chest.
          "I don't want to go alone."

"You won't be
alone," says Charlotte,
moving closer. "Charley—"

          "Billy," Lem interrupts.
          "You know Mama needs you
          more than me. You're better
          at carrying in logs, hushing up the babies."

          Billy swallows, says nothing,
          as if he cannot argue with that,
          but his face looks up at his sisters
          and pleads.

"Go on now, Billy," William Foster says
from behind his wife. "You've got to get started now,
so you get there before dark." Foster takes the shoe
from Billy's hand, gives it over to Lem,
who seems frightened for the smallest of seconds.

          "Please, Lem," Billy says.
          "You can have the shoes.
          I'll keep up without them."

Everyone else is
strapping on shoes, adjusting
blankets and coats.
I turn away,
do the same.
Still.
I hear them.

> Lem's voice, rough and firm,
> "I'll see you in a few days, Billy,
> when I get back with some help."
>
> > Billy gives a hiccup of a sob.
>
> Lem says, "Go on now.
> Go and tell Mama
> we're on our way. Then wait for me
> to come."

I hear other voices seep in
between the brothers,
words of soothing,
words of firmness,
then everyone shuffles around me,
following Father.

We're leaving.
I turn.

> Lem is walking forward, his face
> a mask of stone.
>
> > Billy is walking away, his steps
> > following the prints Dutch Charley makes,
> > but his eyes are turned around,
> > following Lem.

At the First Summit

For all these steps, nothing but snow,
and now — rock, a giant
slick rock that my feet cross carefully,
one step at a time.

In front of me everyone inches on,
heads tucked down, step after step.
I stop, watch them
cross over the mountain, a scraggly line
of cloth bundles, packs on backs, furs.
Like a pack of animals, sniffing at the ground.

Sarah passes me,
sees me eyeing the view, says,
"We're about as near heaven as we can get."

White

It is a view so grand
it hurts.
White,
blinding, piercing, shining
white. A burning white
that catches the light, grows it bigger, sharper,
sends it back into the world,
bright, makes my eyes shut tight.

My eyes will never stop
seeing this white.

Down

Over the summit, there is down,
more mountains, more hills, more snow.
Twice we stop because Charles has to rest
his eyes.   It is difficult to see.
He leads us down. I cannot see a path,
but like the others I follow where he goes.
Pointing and miming,
he stops to check with Luis and Salvador,
but I notice he needs the rest.
Sometimes Father keeps us moving,
while Charles waits behind.

Going Down

Walking down
     is somehow harder
          than walking up,
               sideways we go,
                    falling into the snow
                     with each step,
                         our knees aching, wobbling,
                          we lean into the slope,
                          cling along,
                              as if our bodies want
                               to stay.
                                I think
                                        it would be faster
                                          just to fall.

Fire

Down by a creek,
Luis stops us, tells us we'll camp here.
He and Foster build a fire.
The rest of us gather pine limbs full of needles,
spread them out, make a place to sit, rest.
Father unwraps the beef, carefully slices
each of us a piece, as big as a finger.
I take one for Charles, sit down to wait.

Dark arrives, so does Charles,
a blanket wrapped around him.
He staggers over to the fire.
I take the chunk of beef that I'd held tightly in my hands
over to where he sits.   Up close,
he looks less like a gentleman than I've ever seen,
a sickly, shaking shadow of a man.
When I place it in his hands, I feel
how cold they are.   I'm glad the meat,
tightly gripped by me, was warm.

The Sound of Meat

Next afternoon we're sitting, resting, after a long climb up.
We're catching our breath,
sitting on rocks to spare our legs.
It's quiet except for breathing.

Over from the side, a branch snaps,
Eddy jerks his head around,
raises his finger to his lips, silences
our breaths
as he pulls the rifle at his side
slowly up to his chest.

Another crack.

He rises.

We all turn
toward the sound of movement, footsteps,
something walking slowly.

Eddy raises his gun. We
wait, holding our breath.
I realize I can't stand up,
move away, fast enough, if it's a bear.
But the fact that it could be
a squirrel — too small to feed us all —
terrifies me more.

Another crack,
closer,
I see Eddy's face
lower to the side of the gun
as he adjusts his arm and then

through the bushes
comes Charles,
out of breath, he staggers in, slumps down
at the base of a tree.

We watch him pant.
Eddy lowers his eyes before he lowers his gun,
and I let out my breath.

Imagine.

He almost shot Charles,
thinking he was food.

The Valley

In the morning I see
the land before us stretches
wide,   flat,   plain,   smooth.
Spots below — brown, gray, green —
tiny places   where there is   no snow.
Seeing that is a push,   gets me started,
my feet move so much faster than yesterday,
I find I'm in the front   with Father and Salvador.
As the day goes on, the distance between us in the line grows
until Eddy and Amanda are tiny specks behind me
and Charles — I cannot see at all.

And then

It starts to snow.

Snow

Big, fat flakes
fall all day
on our faces,
on our shoulders,
on our backs,
on our paths,
on,   on,   on,   on.

By the time we stop for the night,
we're heavy from the weight of it,
feet full of frozen pain.
Jay and Eddy have beards coated now with white,
making them appear older than even Father.

Charles is the last to struggle in.
He was so far behind.
Only seconds after he sits down, Eddy
turns to him, says, "How much farther?
You said we'd be there by now."
I wrinkle up my face, shake my head,
but Father beats me to speaking. "No, Eddy.
Mr. Stanton said six days. It's only been four."
Charles is so busy breathing,
so busy closing his eyes, moving his feet
closer to the fire, he doesn't say a word.
"Still," says Eddy, no attempt to hide his anger.
"There are more hills beyond this valley.
Not at all as you described."

Charles says nothing,
but his body shakes, his breath rattles,
bursts from his chest, in and out, in and out.
And somehow, this is worse.

Charles

In the morning, Father speaks to Charles, where he's sitting,
propped up by a tree,
then turns, motions everyone on,
Luis and Salvador at his side.
As they leave the campsite, one by one,
everyone nods to Charles,
who nods back, politely,
his hair carefully smoothed over to the side.
I notice how quickly everyone
turns away. I watch them moving on.
I see Charles is not rising to stand.

"Better get a move on," I say,
when I'm standing right before him.

                    "I am coming soon," he says.

My heart starts to pump faster in my chest
as if it realizes what my brain has not yet.

"Do you want some help up?" I ask.
I offer my hand.
                        His eyes move to it — gloved, ragged,
                        fingers stretched down toward him.
                        He tilts his head to the side,
                        as if examining my hand from another angle.
                        Just when I'm about to pull it back,
                        he reaches out,
                        takes the tips of my fingers in his own,
                        gently, as if one of us is fragile.
I am not moving.
Beside us people are walking past.
I watch the rims of Charles's round eyes
fill up with tears.

                        "Mary Ann,"
                        he says.
I pull away my hand,
take in some shaky breaths.
"So you'll be along," I say.
"After you've rested a bit more."
I'm looking down,
not into his eyes,   I see him
slowly lower his hand.

"Mary Ann." It's Jay.
I turn. He stands there, with Sarah,
in the path the others made,
and I see the others have all gone.
"It's time to go."
His arm is pointing ahead.
Sarah's eyes are down.

I turn to Charles.   His hands are busy now,
                             shuffling in his pocket,
                             pulling out his pipe.

"Mary Ann."
Jay again.

I say nothing more to Charles,
simply step to the side, onto the path
behind where Jay and Sarah stand.
They turn, begin to walk.   I follow
for six steps, before I stop
and look back.
                        Charles is still
                        against the tree,
                        sitting on the cold ground.

I can see his elbow, the back of his head,
the outline of his knee,
and the smoke
from his pipe
as it floats
softly up
and away.

The Last of It

The snow fell
all day again. We stop
earlier than usual, set up camp.

Father pulls out the meat from his sack,
a chunk of beef that could easily fit
inside a coffee mug.
                    "This is the last of it," he says quietly.

Even though it was something we all knew,
I feel fear squeeze my chest.
He kneels down, slices it into fifteen equal parts,
holds them out in his hand.
I take mine, put it in my mouth, blocking out
all thoughts, eat it all at once, without thinking.
Dwelling is not a place to live.

When everyone has finished, I see Father
rewrap the cloth, tuck it under the pine tree where he sits.
                    "For Charles," he says.

The Next Day

The day comes and goes.

We stay in our circle around the fire

while the snow continues to fall,

turning our hair, our faces, white,

as though years sink into our bodies in the course of this one day.

Charles never comes.

Moving

The next day Father rouses us,
       his commanding presence somewhat watered down.
We walk, slowly, heavily, through a deep valley,
Father setting a pace that is slow, wandering.
                 I hear Eddy say, ". . . isn't what he said . . ."
             I hear Foster say, ". . . looks all wrong . . ."

I see Father talking to the Indians, see them
shake their heads, glance away,
see Father, his eyes sunken in, turn to Jay,   say it.

          "We're lost."

And then it rains

hard rain
cold rain

all night
all day

little walking
no food

no idea   where
to go

Food

So cold,

walking in the rain,

but I don't dream of warm.

All I can think about

is food.

I look around me, everywhere,

searching for something alive

something we can kill, eat.

We all look, search.

But the only thing alive

is us.

No Fire

Before the day ends, the rain turns
to snow, somehow thicker,
somehow colder, somehow even worse.

We stop before night falls, try to build a fire,
but everything is damp, the wood, the ground,
ourselves,   even the trees shiver.
In the end, Father
tells us to sit together in a circle,
feet together in the middle.
Foster drapes some blankets
over us and we turn ourselves
into a tent, we sit
tightly together
and wait.

Sarah and Jay

She looks at him,
        shame,

as though she's sorry
she dragged him into this.

He looks at her,
        shame,

sorry
he cannot protect her.

All that sorry
between them,

but there is room
for relief too,

relief
they are together.

Talk

The snow falls, heavy on our blankets.
The winds howl.
We sit as close together as we can. There is
talk.

    "We should go back."   "To camp?"
"We've nothing left to eat."   "They don't have much more there."
    "Maybe rescuers have come by now."   "Maybe
they're all right."   "We couldn't find the way."
"... follow our tracks ..."   "... covered in snow ..."
    "He said 'No turning back.'"

        Beside me, Father says nothing, only shivers.
        His eyes are closed; his breaths are quick, shallow.
        I look on his other side
        to Sarah, but she is listening to Jay.
            "We have to find some food."

"... animals in the woods ..."   "... haven't seen a thing ..."
    "... must be something here alive ..."
            "There is only us."

The snow falls, heavy on our blankets.
The winds howl.
We shiver and shake, wait
for it all to end.

There is crying.   There is praying.
    Oh, God, make it stop.

Father is quiet through it all.

Lem Murphy

It's getting louder now, his muttering.
I can make out the words.

marmalade on toast   buttered bread

apples pulled from the tree,   baked

into pies,   crispy apple fritters

mashed potatoes   gravy   green

beans with pork   corn bread

fish dipped in meal   and fried

in a deep skillet   soup

I can't decide if I want
him to stop or not.

Patrick Dolan

His words are thick with Irish curves,
yelling at his ma,
louder and louder,
he starts to flail, thrash,
my feet are thumped,
the blanket behind me loses its tautness.
Cold crawls in.
Eddy moves toward him,
tries to calm him down.
"Mr. Dolan," Foster cries.
"Put your coat on."
But there is only more cursing, more thrashing.
I feel the blankets shift, see the snow.
"Get inside," Eddy yells.
He and Foster wrestle with Mr. Dolan.
I listen as his mind spins.
I try to keep mine still.

Sleep

In and out of sleep, wake,
I go, stay

dark
cold
night
everyone the same

someone counts the days
says it's Christmas Eve

or maybe that's a dream
Sarah and Jay huddle together
Amanda sobs so loud
Salvador's teeth chatter, a clicking rhythm,
a clock gone mad

next to me, Father,
Father is saying

something

What Father Says

                Mary Ann stay alive
            do not be afraid
                        of anything
        that would keep you
        from dying
                    Mary Ann
            stay alive
            think of Mother
                and the little ones who need
        someone to find help

                think of Frank

                Mary Ann

            stay alive

Father

If there was a final moment,
last glance,
thick sigh as all the air left his lungs
for good,
I missed it,
huddled next to him
next to everyone,
in this dizzy state of waking sleep

I only know he was shivering

and now he's not

The Rest of the Night

everything blurs

around me

dead people

live people

snow   blows

cold

cold

talking

singing

don't know

what's real

asleep

awake

make it stop

oh god

end it

Light

at some point the dark
goes away
the light comes
there are no more prayers, cries,
moans to be heard,
only the wind and the snow around us

some of us are dead

all of us are still

The Dead

Antonio   Lem   Patrick   Father

Four bodies unmoving.

We drag them out onto the snow
and then
make our tent again.

Christmas Day

Another day of snow, wind, cold.
Another day without a fire.
We are so close together
that our thoughts have no room to bounce around,
so they pass from one mind to another
food   *food*   *meat*   *food*
until they land on a tongue,
find their way to air.

"There is something we could eat."

something

we could eat it

          oh god
      we could

there's flesh there   like with the bear
                  the beef
              it's meat
    we could eat it

      oh god   we could

Thoughts

Thoughts   words
rattle around   in this tent
  unhinged.

We could do that.
We could.
It would keep us alive.

. . . but our souls . . .   . . . God would understand . . .
* . . . Think of the people at camp . . .   . . . our families . . .*
. . . their families . . .   . . . God . . .   . . . oh, God . . .
* . . . But Mr. Dolan . . .   . . . Mr. Graves . . .   . . . disrespect . . .*
*   . . . waste the meat . . .*

My own thought cannot stay still:
Father wanted us to live.

Deciding

Foster says he's going to do it.

He's going out there, going to
cut into Mr. Dolan.

Charlotte, his wife, moans, twists her hands.
"Not Lem," she says. "Just not Lem."

"Not for you," says Eddy. "Not for either of you."

Charlotte and her sister squeeze their hands together.
Their faces twist, jerk.

Sarah has horror on her face,
so I tuck away mine,
try to give her a nod.

"We'll stay away from kin," says Jay,
drawing his arm tighter around Sarah,
who blinks now, over and over, as if she cannot stop.

Amanda stands up, says, "We'll all go. Everyone.
Everyone should help."

I look around at the faces, see
the agonizing dread because it's clear
this thing
will be done.

Only Luis and Salvador seem numb
to all this talk.   They don't know
what we're about to do.

Meat

I   help Jay drag Antonio's body underneath a tree.
I   pull off his coat, his boots, his shirts.

Sarah turns her head. Jay takes
the dead man's hat, places it
gently in the snow, gets out
his knife. I finger the blackened
hems of my sleeve.

      I   turn off my brain,
            shut off my thoughts,
            watch Jay cut into the arms,
                    the legs,
                    the middle.
      I   do not think of Eddy and Foster behind me
                    with Father.
      I   take the meat from Jay,
            put it in a sack.

Cold

We build a fire,
there is no heat.

Amanda slices meat,
lays it out to dry,

Foster puts the rest on a skillet
over the flames.

We all sit, wait,
shamefully hungry,

except Salvador and Luis
who've moved over, revolted,

afraid,
under a tree.

Their fire looks warmer.
But they have no food.

I Eat

I don't look at it in my hand
  don't wait for it to cool
or for me to take in the smell,
                  the sight,
                  the thought of what I hold,
     I put it in
   my mouth,   chew

two more days

two more days we stay here
while the meat dries
my clothes dry
my soul dries

my stomach fills

Time to Move

We can't stay
at this awful place.
Time to move. But we're surrounded
by trees, snow, hills. No path in sight.

>   Charlotte speaks up. "I think
>   we should go back." Her sister nods.
>   "We can retrace our steps, get to the others."

Everyone is silent, looking down,
away. I scan their faces,
think they all agree.

"We won't be able to find
our tracks," I say. "The rain,
the snow, they'll all be covered up."

>   "I know which way we came," says Foster.
>   "I can get us there." Charlotte nods again.

>   "They might have had help
>   arrive by now," Frances says.
>   "It might be best if we go back
>   so we can be rescued too."

My whole body clenches
together because the idea of going back
to the cabin, out of the wind, out of the wet,
where Mother is, Mother
who makes sure no one starves.
Oh, I want to say yes.

>   Luis steps forward.
>   "We go on. We keep going.

To California." He points
in a direction that I do not know is west.
Everyone else looks away, at each other.
Luis and Salvador strap on their shoes,
gather up their things.
Sarah is biting
her lip, watching Jay. I say,
"I'm going with them."
I look at Luis and Salvador.
"I'm not going to be one more mouth
to feed for my mother."

Charlotte isn't nodding now.
She looks down, with the others, at the snow.
I strap on my shoes.

      "We're going too," says Sarah,
      moving toward me. Jay
      follows his wife. Amanda
      walks to stand beside me, starts
      strapping on a shoe.

Slowly the others do the same,
take out their shoes, strap them on,
place their eyes on Luis and Salvador, hoping
they can get us out of these woods, out of this place,
out of this winter.

Walking

Walking again.
Up a canyon steep enough
to push us off the side.
My head feels   better.
My stomach   better.
My body   presses on.
We climb up
       up
       up until I can see the valley below us,
              the valley that might be
                California.

Grass

One day climbing up the canyon;
one day climbing down.
We take off the snowshoes
because of the rocks, they cut into our feet,
which bleed. We stop to wrap them,
our tattered feet, busted shoes,
wrap them with rags, cloth we tore
from the clothing of the dead.
My heels need more cover, there's skin
still showing through. I bite into
the bottom of my dress,
rip it with my teeth,
tear off a strip with my hands.
The fabric is stiff again—
not from newness, but from
something else, something that won't let it bend.
I wrap it round my ankle, underneath my feet.

Weak from no food,
Salvador and Luis trail behind.

When we stop, at the bottom, there is grass,
prickly, stiff, cold grass.
I run my fingers over it,
blink, to make sure
it is real.

At Camp

Around the fire, on the grass, we eat
the last of the meat.

No one speaks.
Everyone looks

around.

The Next Day

There is more walking,
grass,   hills,   rocks.
We have no landmark to search for, no map, no sense
of where to head.   Our guides are lost,
dazed, weak, slow. They trail behind.
In return, we start to lag.
Not because we're waiting
for them to catch up, but because
we don't want to leave them behind.

Another Day

Another day of walking
            of no food.

Hunger pains come
faster, sharper, meaner.

Jay moves slowly,
weakly, falls behind.

There is talk.

"The Indians are dying . . ."   ". . . moving slow . . ."
        ". . . won't be able to make it
much longer . . ."   ". . . don't have a soul . . ."
                ". . . like a lame horse that sometimes needs
                        to be relieved of its suffering . . ."

While the Others Sleep

I go to the other fire—small,
dying out—where the Indians lie away
from what we've become.

I shake them awake, try to find
words they'll understand.

"Go.   You need to go."

I shake them,
point,
use my hands,
use my face.

"The others . . . they want . . ."
I look from the others to these men.
I peek down at their chests.
I can't act this out
but they don't need it.
They see my face.   I see theirs
widen in the terror of understanding.

They creep away
as I walk to the fire
lie down, curl into a ball, recoil
at the stench of my dress.

No Indians

The next morning, no one speaks
to me. I don't care.   My head
throbs, my feet sting, my whole body aches.

Eddy takes the lead, veers
us over ground we've covered.
His gun is out as if he's
hunting game.

Tracking

We walk
without speaking, follow Eddy
wherever he leads,
no clear path today,
through bushes today,
through thick groups of trees,
through and through.
Sometimes we see tracks. Sometimes
we see blood.

Tracked

It is dusk when we find them,
crouched under a bush,
starved, shaking,
bloodied feet twitching in the limbs.

They say nothing,
just moan, twitch, close their eyes,
and so neither do I.

I don't speak
when Eddy takes a breath, loads his gun, and

shoots them.

one at a time.

numb

i feel nothing
not my fingers
or my toes
or my thighs
or my neck
or my cheeks
or my tongue

or the warmth

eddy places in my hand

or the taste of it

as it brushes past my lips

into my mouth

down deep

inside me

i feel nothing

We Walk

We walk.
      I think of the river at home—how it smelled
         like moss and wet and mud, sounded
         like wind and dripping rocks.

We walk.
      I think about summer in the wagon, when
         discomfort was the hardest thing to bear.

We walk.
      I think of Father wanting adventure, wanting
         California.   I think of Mother
         in that cabin, unaware he's gone.

We walk.
      I wonder if they're out of food,
         what they've eaten.

Jay and Sarah

It takes longer to walk in a pair,
using your shoulders to hold up more arms than two.

Jay struggles, his legs merely drag, shuffle
along in the snow. Sarah pushes him through.

    I am weak.
But I am one.

My feet burn
with numbness. I cannot make them stay

in the snow, stay
with Sarah and Jay,

so I drift ahead.

Eddy and I

Walking on it's Eddy and I
   and white, trees, snow, slopes,
      just Eddy and I
        and the sun,
           giving the white bright light,
          just Eddy and I
        looking for life,
          searching for help,
         walking on,
           just Eddy and I
             scanning the ground for tracks,
                    looking for meat,
                        something to kill,
                  something to eat,
           just Eddy and I
         and his gun.

Our Eyes

our eyes search
every branch   every limb   every bit of fallen snow
search for tracks   brush bedded down   greenery that's been eaten
we are hunting   tracking   following a trail of   something
anything   that moves   with flesh   to eat
our eyes scan the white   ignore the burn
search   search   search
now and again I look at him   he looks at me
I feel the frantic in my eyes   see the wild in his
like animals   stalking   hungry
only he   holds a gun

Signs

Eddy shows me a low branch,
rubbed free of bark, tells me
to search for more. We split up,
I call to him moments later, tell him
I've seen one.
We both move in that direction
until Eddy shows me a place
where the snow's been packed down,
under a tree, branches and limbs pressed to the ground.
We find a pile of small black pellets,
size of seeds. We climb up
a bank and see it.
A deer.

The Deer

Its ears are pointed straight up,
ready to hear anything.

It springs up
for a moment on its hind legs
to reach the branch above it,

dainty legs,
pointed face,
slender neck,
            so thin,
            so graceful.

But what a belly,
        so thick,
        so full.
I watch it eat,
        chew,
            fill its mouth
            again and again.

One Shot

Eddy grips the gun
so tight
it shakes.
One bullet,
one shot,
one chance to eat.
Don't miss.

Don't miss.

Don't miss.
I close my eyes tight,
can't watch.
He takes in a breath,
mutters something soft
in the tone of a plea,
lets out a heavy, steady exhale, then

!

The shot rings out,
fills the canyon with its sound.
At first all I hear is its echo,

but then I hear
the quick crunching steps of a deer
running away.

The Chase

"Come on," Eddy says.
He pulls on my arm, pulls me up to a stand.

> "What happened?" I say.
> There is no deer.
> "You missed?"

Eddy is over the rock we'd crouched behind,
over the fallen tree in front of it,
slinging the gun over his shoulder,
moving quickly ahead.
"Come on," he says,
without glancing back.
"It went this way."
Then he's off
through a clearing in the trees.

> I follow him, slowly,
> no longer fueled by hope,
> into the trees
> where I see   blood.

Blood

There — on a leaf,

                              there — on the ground,

      a splattered trail of drops

          that lead   —   oh, God   —   he hit it.

We spread out, Eddy and I,

scanning the ground, the trees, the bushes

         for tracks, for blood,

             calling out to each other

when we see which way she went.

"Here."   "Over here."   "I've found a mark."

              A trail in the snow of hooves

     running quickly,   dragging slightly,

   dots of red   on white   splattered between.

We run through the woods,

        follow a path she left for us.

All the while I think   *Thank God for snow.*

All the while I think   *I can taste her.*

All the while I think   *Die. Die.*
                         Hurry up and die.

Where We Find Her

Out of breath,
    tired,
        we stumble into a clearing
            where the sun is setting
                over a pile of brush
                    where the trail stops,
                        we see her,
                            curled up and dying,
                      she sees us,
                where her trail has stopped,
            under a pile of brush,
        where the sun is setting,
      where she has stumbled into a clearing,
    tired,
out of breath.

We Did Not Wait

We did not wait
    to haul it to camp.
We did not wait
    for the others.
We did not wait
    to build a fire.
We did not wait
    even for her to finish dying.

      Eddy sliced her open.
      We filled our mouths.

Dark

It is too dark to find our way
back to the others.
So Eddy builds a fire.
We sit down beside the deer,
who lies between us.
I reach over, fold over her skin,
tuck her meat neatly up inside.
I move behind her, so I can lay my head across her side,
use her body as a pillow. Her blood
seeps into the fabric on my shoulders.
She is still warm.

The Next Day

We retrace our steps,
our path now revealed in its lengthy meandering,
spend all of the morning, most of the day
hauling the doe in pieces,
chunks of meat in Eddy's sack, the hide folded up in mine,
the heart in my stomach, the liver in his,
finding our way to the others.
With food in my belly, I do not mind the walk.

I worry when we do not meet them on the path,
that the sound of the shot
did not call them to us.

But ahead I see the tree
that braces up another, fallen on its side,
smoke sneaking up between them.

I see figures huddled around
that do not get up to greet us,
that do not even look our way,
their eyes intent upon

the meat

over the fire.

Sarah

My heart has only time enough to gulp, not even time to
properly pound out a panic,
before I hear her.
"Mary Ann! You're alive!"

I swivel, see her — standing up beside a tree,
a ways away from the others — all alone.

I walk toward where she stands,
arms outstretched, take in her face,
sunken in with empty, and I know.

> "Oh, no," I say. "Where's Jay?"
> before I can stop myself from asking.
> I look at where the others gather,
> where Eddy approaches,
> but Sarah grabs my arms, pulls me
> around to face her.

"I couldn't stop them," she says.
"But I can't do it myself.
Mary Ann. I can't do it. I can't."

> "They killed him? Who —?"

"No, sister. No."
Sarah shakes her head, something falls
from her hair. "No one killed him.
No."   She grips me tighter.

"It was last night, while he slept . . .
I felt him go . . . just
stopped breathing . . ."
She closes her eyes.
"I wanted to go

with him. I lay there, curled up beside him,
wrapped his arm around me,
closed my eyes, told my heart to stop.
It didn't work.
When morning came, my eyes opened,
even though I wish they hadn't."

She stops, lets go of my arms,
leans against the tree.
"You should go over there now, Mary Ann,
get something to eat . . . before it's all gone . . ."

I shake my head a little, try to rattle out
what I've heard.
I drop the sack in front of me,
pull out a hunk of meat.
Sarah recoils. "It's deer," I say quickly.
"Eddy shot a deer."

Her eyes fix on the meat.
"The shot . . . I heard the shot
last night . . . I thought . . ."

That hangs there between us until I say,
"Let's go cook this a bit over the fire."
I turn toward the others,
but Sarah grabs me again, shakes her head.
"You go, Mary Ann. I'll . . . I'll wait here . . ."

She turns away from me,
away from where the others camp,
away from where her husband
has been ripped apart
over the fire.

Alone

Sarah walks alone now
but no faster than when she walked underneath Jay's arms.
In fact she's somehow slower, as though something even heavier
weighs down upon her with each step,
as though going forward is too much,
too hard, too pointless, as though all she wants to do
is stop.

Hills

These are hills, not mountains,
not difficult to climb,
just enough land popping up from the ground
to block our path, block our way,
block our view.

If only God
would swipe them all away with his hand,
then we'd be able to see
where we are going.

Circles

we are walking in circles
we turn left sometimes
we turn right sometimes
but there's never any sign we're headed for anything
nothing to eat   nothing to see
sometimes we meet our footprints and turn away in shame
nothing to see   nothing to eat
never any sign we're headed for anything
sometimes we turn left
sometimes we turn right
we are walking in circles

No Rest

Sarah is tired, walking too slow,
stopping too much.
                    Twice Eddy asks if she's well.
            Twice Amanda turns to see if she's still going.
Twice I catch Foster and his wife, whispering, peering at Sarah.

"Come on," I tell her, taking her arm
when she leans against a tree.
                    "You go," she says, her hand to her chest
                    while she sucks in gulps of air. "I'll be right on."

"No," I say.
I place my hand on her elbow,
pull her arm toward me.
                    "Mary Ann!" She shakes her head. "I'm fine.
                    Really. I only need a minute's rest."

I step into her,
move my grip up her arm.
"You can't rest here," I hiss,
my words low and hard.
"They're watching you, Sarah.
You've got to keep moving."

                    "But it was—"

I yank her arm, spin her around.
"Don't let them think you're weak."

                    She grunts in protest
but from the side of my eye I see
her face suddenly blink in horror and I know she understands.

This Land

this land
has eaten
my feet
chewed them
ripped them
cut them

they bleed
into land
that drinks
them up

but it is never full

My Eyes

My eyes are seared by bright,
                can't shut out the light.
Open, they take in shapes so bright
that when I close my eyes tight,
the shapes are still there, burnt into my sight,
dark switched with light.

I can't unsee them.

  can't unsee all this.

Apart

we are   no longer   a group   all walking   apart clustered
fanning out   wandering but   I make   sure Sarah   is in
my sight   with me   that we   are together   even when
we stop   by a tree   because we   cannot walk
anymore even   when dark   sets in   and I   hear her

say *this*   *is it*   *Mary Ann*   *this is*   *where we're*
going to   *die* I   don't want   to move
but I   do I   sit up   find her   face put   it in
my hands   lay it   on my   chest dress   so thin   I tuck
her cold   feet under   my skirts
I feel   her bones   before I

say *we'll*   *get through*   *this you'll*
see then   *it will*   *be just*

a story   *to tell*

In and Out

              in and out
         i am
              in and out
         i fade
      the tree
                 the snow
            in and out
       the sun
                  the dark
    in
            and out
                        then
                 hands
            a face
                 in and out
       i'm dragged
  in and out
                 across snow
                    in and out
         carried
                 cold
       in and out
i see
            smoke from a chimney

    a light

            my head bumps against a door

Spring
1847

Four Months Later
Sutter's Fort, California

A New Quilt

I'm stitching
        a new quilt
                from scraps of cloth
that dangled from our bodies
when we arrived, mostly gray,
but there's a bit of green I found, still bright,
from underneath a collar.
                                           I stitch

Sarah comes, tells me
the rescuers have left, taking
our letters to Mother.   I stitch
Amanda comes, tells me
Bill has gone with them, gone to get
Harriet, Eliza, Mother, the others.   I stitch,
my feet propped up before me,
trying to heal.

I'm stitching
        a new quilt
                when Will arrives,
Eleanor, Lovina, looking like ghosts of my family,
walking through the door, looking past me to
bread.   I stitch
while they eat and heal,   days of rest.
                                                I stitch

while they tell me the snow was too high
for the little ones to walk out
of the camp, so Mother stayed with them.   I stitch
while Amanda hears that Harriet has died.

                                              I stitch

with more scraps to add,
more dingy gray,
but now a touch of blue, a streak of yellow.
Days come and come,
the quilt grows and grows.

I'm stitching
                a new quilt
                                from scraps of the clothes
Mother made us for the journey
when Nancy,
                thin and small,
                                steps into the house, holding Eliza,
                                Jonathan trailing behind,

when the men with them, Bill and others, tell me Mother

                                left the cabin, carrying Eliza,
                        dragging Nancy, Jonathan, Frank behind her,
                        the snow still too deep for those little legs,
                                and she only had two arms.

                They came to a place where the rescuers stopped
                to tell them they couldn't keep walking that slow.
                                So she stayed,
                        with the little ones, waiting for someone
                                to come back.

                                Bill found them, days later.

I'm stitching
                    a new quilt
                                        nothing like the other one,
the red one,
                    the journey one,
                                        that lies in the mountains,
on the snow,
                    the cold,
                                        the ground,
wrapped around
                    Frank's body,
                                        inside Mother's arms.

I'm stitching
        a new quilt
                using all the scraps of cloth
so when I'm finished
            there will be
                no scraps of gray behind.

I'm stitching
        a new quilt
               joining layers together,
fabric pulled taut in the hoop,
I don't quilt it with a pattern, with lines or circles, no.
Instead I quilt it with pictures.
A bear here. A deer.
A tree with thick, strong limbs.

I'm stitching
           on my quilt
                        quilting it together,
while Sarah gathers up children in the fort,
teaches them to read.
She talks of better things,
warmer weather, fruits she finds,
anything but winter.

                I stay away from that.
                My eyes still burn
                with a brightness that will never go away,
                and it hurts to pretend all day
                that I haven't just come awake
                from a nightmare so real my feet bleed.

I'm stitching
           on my quilt
                      binding it together,
when one of the rescuers,
           young Edward Pyle,
                       takes to spending time with me.

                                          I stitch.

He watches me sew, lets me talk —
        about the hunger, about the cold,
        about eating what we ate.
He never flinches or looks away.
He lets me speak
without offering up silly hushing words
like the others do around here. "There, there, now."
        "Best to forget about it."   "Best to move on."
        "God has seen you through."
He simply nods and listens.

                                          I stitch.

He seems to understand I don't want to hear this,
don't want to see the others from this winter,
don't want to be around anyone at all.
He understands I cannot cry.
My eyes will not make tears.
And one day, as we're sitting here,
him sharpening an ax and me stitching on the quilt,
I look up at him, say, "Should we get married, then?"
He doesn't even stop rubbing the blade on the stone,
just looks up to meet my eyes
long enough to say yes.
And so it is.

I stitch
   until
      the quilt is finished.

I hold it up for all to see.
Amanda and Lovina smile,
   Sarah's eyes begin to tear.
      Will puts down Jay's fiddle, which
      he's learning to play, and nods.

Eleanor tells me, "It's the loveliest quilt I've seen."

It is a field of gray,
   a wall of worn-out worry,
      patches and patches
      of sewn-together sorrow.
But that is only a background,
on top there is a rainbow of life,
   a tapestry of creatures,
      a forest of hope,

      for I used brightly colored threads.

It is soft,
   already worn,
      but it is strong, finely stitched;
      it will hold up nicely.

      It is meant to endure.

Epilogue

Mary Ann Graves married Edward Pyle on May 16, 1847, at Sutter's Fort.

One year later, he was murdered. When a man named Antonio Valencia was found guilty of the murder and sentenced to death, Mary Ann cooked and delivered meals to him while he was in jail. She later said it was because she wanted to make sure he stayed alive long enough to be hanged.

In 1851, she married again, to James Thomas Clarke, and together they had seven children.

She enjoyed smoking a pipe.

She had problems with her eyes for the rest of her life.

Author's Note

Historical fiction requires a careful balance of real and embellished, a base of facts with a sprinkling of supposition and imagination. Although I've changed a few names to simplify the cast of characters for the reader (there were a lot of men named William), the events that unfold in this story all happened.

Mary Ann Graves was a real person. She and her family left their home near Lacon, Illinois, in April 1846 and traveled 1,700 miles west, with the hope of settling in California. On November 1, Mary Ann's twentieth birthday, they were stopped in their tracks by a snowstorm that lasted for days. The snow didn't melt until spring. They were starving. Trapped. And less than a hundred miles from their destination.

When Mary Ann and sixteen others set out with snowshoes on December 16, they were leaving the camp with the idea that someone had to go for help. The walk should have taken them six days, but they were lost in the snow, and thirty-two days later, when they were completely emaciated, confused, out of food, with ruined feet, very tattered clothes, and empty stomachs, one of them, William Eddy, stumbled into a cabin on a ranch owned by William Johnson. The people inside couldn't believe the state of the man before them or the tale he told. They quickly went out into the night, retraced his steps by the blood his feet had left behind, and found Mary Ann and Sarah and the others, all in varying states of consciousness. They had been wandering in circles for some time, eighteen miles away from help they could not find.

Rescue parties were soon organized for the others back at the lake. Men from the nearby fort set out with supplies. Some turned around in the middle of their journey, forfeiting their pay, because they saw the difficulty of the task. Several people were rescued. But it was primarily women and children left at that point, and the high snow made it difficult for the small children to walk, meaning many more died before help could reach them, or they died along the journey out. In all, of the eighty-one people trapped in the mountains, only forty-five were alive when spring finally arrived.

There were so many wagon trains going west that year. What went wrong with the Donner Party? A combination of things, including a very rainy spring, stops and delays along the way, and an early, snowy winter. (If the snow had held off by just twenty-four hours, in fact, Mary Ann and her family likely would have been able to cross over the mountain.) But the biggest factor in their delay was probably that they chose to take a different route—the Hastings cutoff—which took them south of the Great Salt Lake. Though Hastings and others insisted that the route was practicable, the Donner Party discovered it was an arduous passage for wagons. It took them weeks longer to navigate through the Wasatch Mountains, and they were never able to make up the time.

Even though the cannibalism is what most people remember about the Donner Party, I found the other parts of their journey just as captivating. *What is the likelihood that Eliza Donner's recounting of Hastings's note before the desert crossing was real?* Maybe Hastings was traveling back—or sending someone else back—to leave notes along the way. Maybe he was leaving the notes before he crossed himself. Maybe Eliza made it up years later. We just don't know. *Or how about that rumor that Louis Keseberg reveled in the cannibalism so much that he kept a bucket of blood by his bed?* More than one member of the rescue party mentioned it. Would they make it up? Keseberg denied it. . . . *Or how about those coins Mrs. Graves so carefully hid away from everyone? What happened to those?* (She buried them somewhere during her attempt to walk out after they became too heavy to carry. Decades later, it appears they were dug up and some of them were shared with her descendants.)

I have always been captivated by stories of survival. I wanted to write the story of Mary Ann Graves because it's a story about what a person will do and endure in order to survive. The pioneers who journeyed west during this time were certainly brave and adventurous. They were also, of course, trespassing on and invading land that belonged to people who were already living there. Though many Native American people were helpful and friendly to pioneers, many others naturally tried to defend their land and sources of food. What some people think of as a proud period in our history others rightly consider tragic.

The story of the Donner Party is a powerful one. It's a story that makes us consider what choices we would make if we were on the brink of death. This group of families and the trials they faced became legendary and etched for them a permanent place in our history tales. Truckee Lake, where Mary Ann's family spent the winter, is now called Donner Lake, though, ironically, the Donner family was camped farther away, at Alder Creek. We're still captivated by this story, more than a century later, because it's full of elements we can relate to, even today. Hard feelings, arguments, murder, thievery, heartbreaking acts of charity, and yes — romance.

Mary Ann was often called the belle of the Donner Party. There have been stories that she was romantically linked to John Snyder, her family's teamster, who was killed by James Reed, and even conjecture that Charles Stanton was smitten with her, too. None of that has been verified as fact.

Mary Ann herself vehemently denied a romantic link to anyone. Thirty years later, a newspaper editor named C. F. McGlashan published the story of the Donner Party, including hints of romance for Mary Ann. She said to him in a letter that "it was possible that such a company did exist and without a romance, 'twas all real life of a sterner type."[1]

Of all her surviving letters about that winter, this letter stood out in its tone and forcefulness. Perhaps that's because it's true there was no romance. Or perhaps these are the words of someone who's endured loss in love and life and doesn't want to think of it again. Her brother, much more candid on all matters about that winter, and who Mary Ann herself said was honest in recounting what happened to them on that journey, had this to say to McGlashan about Mary Ann's possible liaisons: "As to your 'romance,' I suppose it is as true as the majority of them. But I don't altogether approve of it in that place. Gossip always knows more about such things than the principles [sic] themselves."[2]

In my research, I saw that Mary Ann was beautiful, strong, resourceful, determined, and permanently scarred by what she endured on this trip. I've tried to imagine how it might have gone for her. But in the end, it's only my imagination.

[1] July 18, 1879, letter to C. F. McGlashan from Mary Ann Graves
[2] March 30, 1879, letter to C. F. McGlashan from W. C. Graves

Mary Ann Graves, 1879

The Donner Party

The following is a list of those people who either were part of the group at the time the Graves family joined up with the Donner Party in August 1846 or who joined the group anytime thereafter. (The list does not include people who died or left the group before this date.) Some ages are confirmed by records, and others are only an approximation, based on Kristin Johnson's *Unfortunate Emigrants: Narratives of the Donner Party* (Logan: Utah State University Press, 1996). Those who survived the journey are listed in plain text; those who perished are listed in *italics*.

Family Groups

Franklin Ward Graves (57)
    Elizabeth Cooper Graves (45)
    Mary Ann Graves (19)
    William Cooper Graves (17)
    Eleanor Graves (14)
    Lovina Graves (12)
    Nancy Graves (9)
    Jonathan Graves (7)
    Franklin Ward Graves Jr. (5)
    Elizabeth Graves (1) Although she was rescued, she died shortly after arriving at Sutter's Fort.
    Jay Fosdick (23)
        Sarah Graves Fosdick (21)

Patrick Breen (51)
    Margaret Bulger Breen (40)
    John Breen (14)
    Edward Breen (13)
    Patrick Breen Jr. (9)
    Simon Preston Breen (8)
    James Frederick Breen (5)
    Peter Breen (3)
    Margaret Isabella Breen (1)

George Donner (62)
    Tamsen Eustis Dozier Donner (44)
    Elitha Cumi Donner (14)
    Leanna Charity Donner (12)
    Frances Eustis Donner (6)
    Georgia Ann Donner (4)
    Eliza Poor Donner (3)

Jacob Donner (65)
    Elizabeth Blue Hook Donner (45)
    Solomon Elijah Hook (14)
    William Hook (12)
    George Donner Jr. (9)
    Mary Donner (7)
    Isaac Donner (5)
    Samuel Donner (4)
    Lewis Donner (3)

William Henry Eddy (28)
    Eleanor Priscilla Eddy (25)
    James Eddy (3)
    Margaret Eddy (1)

Johann Ludwig Christian (Louis) Keseberg (32)
    Elisabeth Philippine Zimmermann Keseberg (23)
    Ada Keseberg (3)
    Louis Keseberg Jr. (1)

William McCutchen (30)
    Amanda Henderson McCutchen (25)
    Harriet McCutchen (1)

Levinah W. Jackson Murphy, widow (36)
    John Landrum Murphy (16)
    Mary Murphy (14)
    Lemuel B. Murphy (12)
    William Green Murphy (10)
    Simon Peter Murphy (8)
        William McFadden Foster (30)
            Sarah Ann Charlotte Murphy Foster (19)
            George Foster (2)
        William M. Pike (25)
            Harriet Frances Murphy Pike (18)
            Naomi Lavina Pike (2)
            Catherine Pike (1)

James Frazier Reed (45)
    Margret Wilson Keyes Backenstoe Reed (32)
    Virginia Elizabeth Backenstoe (13)
    Martha Jane "Patty" Reed (9)
    James Frazier Reed Jr. (6)
    Thomas Keyes Reed (4)

Mr. _____ Wolfinger (?)
    Doris Wolfinger (20)

Unmarried Individuals

Antonio (23), hired on by the Donners at Fort Laramie

Charles Burger "Dutch Charley" (30), teamster for the Donners

John Denton (28), traveled with the Donners

Patrick Dolan (35), friend of the Breens'

Milford Elliott (28), teamster for the Reeds

Luis (?), one of Sutter's vaqueros

Luke Halloran (25), traveled with the Donners

Mr. Hardcoop (60), traveled with the Kesebergs

Walter Herron (27), teamster for the Reeds — went ahead with Reed
   when he was banished

Noah James (20), teamster for the Donners

Joseph Rheinhard (30)

Salvador (?), one of Sutter's vaqueros

Samuel Shoemaker (25), teamster for the Donners

James Smith (25), teamster for the Reeds

John Snyder (25), teamster for the Graveses

Augustus Spitzer (30)

Charles Tyler Stanton (35), traveled with the Donners

Jean Baptiste Trudeau (16), hired on by the Donners at
   Fort Bridger

Baylis Williams (25), worked for the Reeds

Eliza Williams (31), worked for the Reeds

Acknowledgments

Statistically, members of the Donner Party were more likely to survive that winter if they were traveling with their family as opposed to by themselves. This was a difficult book to write, and I couldn't have done it without my own writing family.

First and foremost, I have the greatest writing BrainTrust an author could have. Thank you to Kristin Derwich, Lindsay Eyre, Erin Hagar, Maggie Lehrman, Stefanie Lyons, and Amy Zinn for the constant support, title help, and revision rescues. If I had to be stuck in the mountains all winter with a group of people, I'd pick you.

My agent, Tina Wexler, steered this book in the right direction from the very first scenes. She is savvy about all matters business and poetry. And that is a wonderful combination for me.

Everyone at Candlewick Press works so hard to make good books that matter. I am indebted to the many people who worked on this one, especially Carter Hasegawa and Liz Bicknell, who edited this book with all the care, patience, and wisdom that it needed.

Thank you to the Indiana Arts Commission for awarding me a grant that made it possible for me to retrace the steps Mary Ann Graves took on her journey west.

Huge thanks to Kristin Johnson, Donner Party expert, who weighed in on my retelling and research and offered up ways to make the book better. All mistakes or inaccuracies in this story are my own.

Research is fascinating, readers. It's nice to find someone else who finds it equally so. On that note: to Jarrod, Gustavo, Isaac, and Luís—I'm so sorry for all the Donner Party facts you had to endure over dinner. It's over now. You're welcome.